FIGHTBACK

When Tom Harker gets shot at, there's nothing personal about it, but when he shoots back, things change . . . Walter Viall, the cattle king of Tate Country, has a murky past and doesn't take kindly to strangers meddling in his affairs. He has used intimidation and violence to get the law-abiding town of Laureston exactly where he wants it — and he has no intention of letting anyone get in his way. He remains unchallenged . . . until Tom leads the fightback . . .

Books by Joseph John McGraw
in the Linford Western Library:

SILVEROO

JOSEPH JOHN McGRAW

FIGHTBACK

Complete and Unabridged

LINFORD
Leicester

First published in Great Britain in 2010 by
Robert Hale Limited
London

First Linford Edition
published 2011
by arrangement with
Robert Hale Limited
London

The moral right of the author has been asserted

British Library CIP Data

McGraw, Joseph John.
  Fightback.- -(Linford western library)
  1. Western stories.
  2. Large type books.
  I. Title II. Series
  823.9'2–dc22

ISBN 978–1–4448–0915–2

Published by
F. A. Thorpe (Publishing)
Anstey, Leicestershire

Set by Words & Graphics Ltd.
Anstey, Leicestershire
Printed and bound in Great Britain by
T. J. International Ltd., Padstow, Cornwall

This book is printed on acid-free paper

1

Ambushed

He was a tall man and he rode tall in the saddle. A square jaw, lazy blue eyes that missed nothing that was there to be seen. Which is why he did not see, nor could any right-minded man have expected him to see, the hidden sharpshooter high on the canyon wall.

The first shot took his hat off. The second didn't hit anything except the rock exactly behind the spot where the tall rider's head had been a split second before he'd leaped out of the saddle. His horse shied, snorted and trotted on, riderless.

There was no third shot because the sharpshooter had no target. The tall man had hit the dirt hard, rolled fast and was now crouching behind a boulder. He screwed up his eyes against the sun and scanned the canyon wall above him. His gun was in his hand. The hammer was cocked. There was still nothing to see, nothing to shoot at.

Silence returned to the canyon while the tall man settled down to wait for the sharpshooter to make the next move.

There was nothing personal about the ambush. Tom Harker had never ridden this way before. No one knew he was coming. So he reckoned it was a fixed stake-out. A man posted high on the canyon wall, well hidden from the trail a hundred feet below, put there to stop anyone trying to come through. Or maybe someone in particular. It was a good place for an ambush. One man could hold up a whole army here for a day.

But if it hadn't started personal, it was sure as hell personal now.

Harker turned his head and took in the lie of the land. The boulder was close to the trail but there was no cover to left or right of it. At his back was a stand of mesquite. He risked another peek at the rocks towering over him. He'd been off his guard and the shots had taken him by surprise. Where had the sharpshooter been shooting from? High up, that was for sure. And he had a sense the shot had come from up there, from those rocks opposite and a little way along, but he couldn't be sure, it had happened so fast.

A small stone rattled down the canyon wall. Harker didn't watch it all the way down. He didn't even look at it after it came to rest plumb in the middle of the trail. His kept his eyes on a spot seventy feet up, on the opposite side.

The stone could have been dislodged by a bird or a jackrabbit or maybe a man's foot as he changed position to relieve a touch of cramp or get a better view of the trail below. The kind of man who might have a rifle in his hands, bullets in the spout and a target in his sights.

Harker's concentration was rewarded. There was a glint as of sun on metal, then it was gone. He hadn't imagined it. And it wasn't a bird or a jackrabbit, but it could have been the barrel of a gun. No more stones clattered down from above. But he now had a fix on the position of the sharpshooter high on the wall opposite.

He wanted answers. But first, he had to get out of the jam he was in.

He eased down the hammer on his Colt and holstered it. He backed slowly into the mesquite behind him, crawling on his belly under the branches so they didn't shake and give him away. At the back of it, the canyon wall rose sheer. But a faultline, or maybe a layer of softer stone which had been worn away by the centuries, separated two massive blocks and left a passage several feet deep and wide enough to admit a man.

Carefully, Harker got on his knees then inserted himself into the vertical shaft and began to climb, bracing his shoulders against one wall and pushing up with his legs on the other.

When he had shimmied maybe

twenty feet up, he looked down. His hat was lying in the trail dust ten yards from where he'd been thrown off his horse. Even from this distance, he could make out the hole that had been bored in the centre of the crown. It took a decent hand with a rifle to do that. Unless it was a fluke. But Harker had been around long enough to know that a wise man never bets his life on flukes.

He climbed some more. Forty feet above the trail he reached a ledge. He hauled himself on to it, waited until his breath was no longer sounding like a loco climbing a gradient, and peered cautiously round the rock wall.

His hat hadn't moved from its spot in the middle of the trail. No more stones had fallen down. The only thing he saw now that he couldn't see before was the heel of a boot peeking out from behind a rock twenty feet above and across from him. He pulled his head back, eased the Colt from its holster and took another careful look at that boot. It hadn't moved.

It was an awkward shot from the ledge. His back was against the rock wall and the angle required his right wrist to bend further than nature intended. But he had to take his chance. He might not get another one.

The barrel of the Colt made a barely audible scraping noise against the rock but to Harker it sounded like mountain thunder. He froze. Then he risked another look.

The boot went on not moving. The man with the rifle hadn't heard a thing, hadn't changed position, was still looking the wrong way.

Slowly he edged further over the drop until his arm was free enough to give him a decent shot at that boot. It wouldn't kill his man, but it might slow him down. Anyway, there wasn't much else he could do.

He narrowed his eyes, fought hard to keep his hand still then pulled the trigger.

The crack of the gun echoed like a grenade thrown into a cathedral.

Harker jerked back into his hidey-hole before his man could locate his position and fire back.

But no one shot back. There were no more bombs in churches, only a strangled cry.

Harker risked a look and was in time to see a young fellow, probably no more than twenty, in a brightly coloured check shirt standing upright, his arms flailing as he strove to keep his balance.

The shot hadn't hit the boot he had seen. There was no trace of blood. But it had been close enough to startle the sharpshooter, catch him off his guard and make him lose his footing.

Harker thought about taking a second shot but not for long. He wasn't the sort who fired at sitting targets. The man in the check shirt dropped his rifle, which bounced off the canyon's rocky walls on its way to the trail seventy feet below. For a moment, he hung there, weightless, and then slowly toppled forward and followed it down.

Harker watched him fall all the way,

like a rag-doll dropped by a child, bones breaking against projections and wounds gouged blood-red by rocky spurs. If he wasn't dead before he hit the trail, the impact was enough to snap his neck. The body came to rest with the head lying at an unnatural angle and didn't move.

Harker waited.

He waited. While he waited the body went on not moving. But nothing else stirred either. No answering shot, no sound such as might have been made by another hidden man, a second sharpshooter waiting for him to make a wrong move.

Telling himself he couldn't stay parked on a ledge for ever, he shimmied down to trail level where he waited some more, crouching under the mesquite bush until the motion of the sun moved his hat and the corpse into shadow. Carefully, he sat up, then stood up. Only then did he decide that he was all by himself in the canyon.

The man was already cold. Harker

retrieved his hat and whistled up his horse, which came trotting back to him a few moments later. He climbed into the saddle and rode the couple of hundred yards to the far side of the canyon. There he found what he was looking for: a horse, a sorrel mare, tethered to a stand of cotton-woods. He unhitched the mare and led it back to the place where he'd been shot at, hoisted the body facedown over the horse's back. It shied nervously, spooked by death, by the change in the man who had ridden her there, then settled down. Harker tied the dead man's hands and feet under the horse's belly. While he was so occupied, he had plenty of time to confirm that his shot had missed the man's boot.

'Whoever you are,' muttered Harker, 'I cain't leave you here to be supper for coyotes.'

Leading the sorrel, he rode on, up to the head of the canyon and along the trail which wound its way under the westering sun.

The going was good. The country hereabouts was flat and green and there was plenty of evidence of the hand of man. After an hour or so, he rounded a clump of pines and saw buildings not much more than a mile up ahead.

'Laureston,' he said, and he dug his heels into his mount, which picked up the pace.

As he neared town, he passed a wagon or two and an occasional rider who stared at him, said nothing and kept their distance. Good, law-abiding folk don't take kindly to men leading horses carrying corpses. But Harker hailed one of them:

'I'd be obliged if you'd tell me the whereabouts of the sheriff's office,' he said pleasantly. 'I came across this dead man on the trail and don't know rightly what to do with him.'

Following the directions he was given, Harker rode past the church, a bank, Laureston's only general stores, and Laureston's one hotel and watering hole. When he got to the one-storey building with 'Sheriff's Office' painted over the door, he dismounted, tied both horses to the hitching rail, walked up the steps and stepped inside.

Sheriff Silas Rukatch, sixty, greying, alert, looked up from his chair behind a desk.

'Got something for you, Sheriff,' said Harker pleasantly. 'You'd best come and take a look for yourself.'

Outside on the boardwalk, Sheriff Rukatch lifted his hat, scratched his head and gave a low whistle.

'What do we have here, son?' he asked, nodding with his head to what was slung over the back of the sorrel. 'I'll tell you. What you got there, son, is Zeke Viall,' he said, and then stopped.

'So?'

'Why, he's only Walt Viall's youngest boy! You never heard of Walter Viall?'

'I don't read the papers, I don't go to political meetings, I don't pay much attention to other folks and their doings. Be quicker if you tell me who this Walt Viall is. But first, shouldn't we

11

get this boy inside, off the street, or call the undertaker to take care of him? Don't seem decent us chewing the fat on the porch with a dead body for company.'

Sheriff Rukatch grunted then called to a gang of boys playing jackstones in the dust and told one of them to go fetch Ernest Gutman.

'The boy's my grandson. Gutman's the man that lays out all the corpses roundabouts. Calls himself a mortician.'

Gutman came, nodded to the Sheriff, took a look at the body, sniffed and led the sorrel back to his parlour.

'Gutman don't say much,' said Harker.

He turned to leave but the Sheriff told him to step into his office.

'What's the story, mister?' he said. 'You better make it good because there's important people going to want to know how Walter Viall's boy managed to get himself killed. There ain't no bullet holes in the body. But he looks all broken up, like he got between a buffalo and a boulder. You fall out with Zeke?'

In a few words, Harker told his story.

'So he shot at you and missed, then you shot at him and missed and then Zeke slipped and fell into Mason Canyon? Why would he want to shoot at you?'

'No idea. I was never this way until now. I never saw him before, I never heard of his father. Maybe he was just practising.'

By now a small crowd had gathered outside. They wanted to know what was going on. When the news got around, nobody sobbed or tore their hair or laid down and ate dust out of grief. Mostly the townsfolk stayed pretty cheerful, Harker thought, though he couldn't tell whether it was Zeke or his father who was the unpopular one.

'So who's this Viall?' asked Harker, as the crowd dispersed now that there was nothing to see.

'Walter Viall is a cattleman. Got the

13

biggest spread in Tate County. He came here fifteen years ago, before there was a Laureston to be king of. Behaves like he owns the place and in many ways he does. His word is law. Like some old-time grandee. He don't like people messing with what's his. Zeke was his youngest boy. There are two other brothers, Mikey and Rube. Old Man Viall ain't going to like this, so if I was standing in your boots, I wouldn't stick around too long. A man on his own might find the air of Laureston a mite on the powerful side and catch his death. I got a star on my shirt, but there's only one of me to look after folks' interests. I'd say you've just made a lot of enemies.'

Harker stared at the Sheriff but didn't make a move or open his mouth.

'But if you're thinking of just passing through, you cain't do that neither. I'll need you around for a spell. You witnessed the death. Judge Morton will want to know what you got to say for yourself.'

'Maybe I should have left Zeke to the coyotes. But I ain't just passing through. Ever heard of a man named Billy Boden?'

'Sure. He came here five, six years back.'

'Was he alone?'

'There was a dozen of them. Came about the Government's land licence scheme. The politicians back East passed a law saying a man could pick out a piece of land, register it and then work it. If he didn't work it, he lost it. Most of the men found the picking and registering part easy, but not the working. Of the dozen that came, there's only Billy Boden still on the claim he staked.'

'Was it the work they didn't like? Or was there something else that encouraged them to move on?'

'Meaning?'

'Well,' said Harker. 'I reckon the king of Laureston wouldn't take kindly to a bunch of newcomers muscling in on territory he thought was his already. I'd

15

say a man like that would be very protective of his own interests.'

'There was some talk of men being pushed off their claims. Nothing was ever proved against anybody.'

'What sort of talk?'

'Fences torn up, wells poisoned, breeding cows mauled by dogs without anybody being able to say who them dogs belonged to and how they got anywhere near the cows.'

'So the newcomers raised cattle too,' said Harker thoughtfully. 'No wonder Viall didn't like it.'

'I never said nothing about Viall being behind it. There ain't no proof. You go round saying I marked Walter Viall's name for forcing those men off their legally registered land and I'd have to deny it.'

Harker nodded. He wondered why the sheriff, who struck him as a straight-dealing sort of man, was so cagey about Viall. He found out in the next thirty seconds.

There was a sound of boots on the

wooden boards of the sidewalk and the door of the sheriff's office burst open.

'Where is he?' said a thick-set man with an angry red face, maybe thirty, carrying too much weight. 'Where's the son of a bitch that shot my brother? Is this the man?'

'Nobody shot Zeke, Rube,' said Sheriff Rukatch, 'so there's no cause for you to get riled up the way you are.'

The man glared back furiously. His face was covered with sweat and he was breathing hard.

'So where's my kid brother? Is this the man that shot him?'

'Zeke's over at Gutman's funeral parlour. He's dead, all right, but it was an accident. You go over to Gutman's, check for yourself. Nobody shot Zeke. He fell. Broke his neck. An accident.'

Rube pushed the sheriff to one side and took a swing at Harker.

Harker leaned his head back and Rube's fist met only empty air. The weight he'd put behind the punch spun him round, made him trip over his feet and sent him sprawling on the floor.

If Rube had been mad before, he was now beside himself with rage.

He got up and closed in on Harker. He tried another roundhouse swing which Harker avoided and countered with a straight left to Rube's nose.

'Back off, Rube,' he warned. 'Calm down. There's no need for this, you've got no cause for a quarrel with me.'

But Rube wiped the blood from his nose and came on again, this time poking out a left, which also hit only fresh air, before reaching for his opponent with both arms to pin him in a bear hug.

But he was no match for the tall stranger with the lazy eyes. Harker dodged Rube's arms, rocked his head back with three snappy lefts and a right in quick succession. But instead of pressing home his advantage, he dropped his fists, took a step back and said:

'Cut it out! If you want to talk, we'll talk. I'll buy you a drink.'

But Rube was not in a talking,

drinking mood. With eyes of hate in a face of fury he charged Harker.

This time, Harker stood his ground and struck out a straight right which caught his man clean on the point of the jaw.

Rube went down like a dropped sack.

The silence that filled the room was broken by Harker who turned to Sheriff Rukatch and said:

'So where will I find Billy Boden's place?'

2

Tabitha

Billy Boden had staked out his plot on the floor of a high valley a thousand feet above the plain and ran cattle on it. Bluestone Valley was a couple of hours gentle riding from Laureston. A man could easy walk it in half a day.

Harker glanced up at the sky from which the light was now draining fast. It was too late to go landing on folks. Putting the trip off until morning, he found himself a room for the night in Laureston's only hotel. He stabled his horse then walked down the street to the eating-house he'd been directed to — Ma Kelly's. He ordered meat loaf, corn hash and gravy and ate with appetite.

He finished his coffee, paid the bill and headed back to the hotel through the silky warm dark. He walked into the bar and stood at the counter, minding his own business while he drank a beer before turning in.

'Buy you another?'

The voice at his elbow belonged to a handy-looking man of thirty-five with dark hair and a friendly, handsome, open face.

'A.B. Monkman,' he said. '*Laureston Gazette*. Some folks call me AB, others say Abe.'

'Laureston has its own paper?' said Harker in surprise.

'Sure,' said Abe.

'Hard to believe there's enough going on in a town like this to warrant it. What sort of stories do you print? Weddings, new arrivals in town, fat-stock prices . . . '

' . . . and deaths, natural and unnatural . . . '

'Ah,' said Harker, guessing the reason for Abe's offer of a beer. A newspaper-man's business is news.

' . . . and the many and varied doings

of Walter Viall. So a death in the Viall family is doubly news, and if that death ain't natural, why it's the biggest story there's been roundabouts in the last eight years since I been editor, chief and only reporter, typesetter, book-keeper and vendor of the *Laureston Gazette*. So what happened?'

Abe took out a notebook and a pencil. He licked the end of the pencil and waited expectantly.

'You got back files?' asked Harker, asking his own question instead of answering Abe's.

'Sure. Why d'you want to know?'

'Can I take a peek?'

'What are you looking for?'

'Come on,' said Harker, 'let's go see the files. There's no time like the present.'

Finishing his drink and reaching for his hat, he led the way out through the batwing doors of the saloon into the street.

The offices of the *Laureston Gazette* occupied the ground floor of a clap-board building on the next block. While

Abe lit a couple of lamps, Harker took a look around.

The front office had a roll-top desk, a battered swivel chair and a shelf of reference books. On the walls were framed front pages, some dealing with major episodes of the War, others carrying reports of natural disasters and notable local events. The name of Viall ran through them like a recurring theme.

Abe pulled up a straight-backed chair for Harker then sat himself down at the desk.

'Look, friend,' said Abe, 'you want to look at back numbers of the *Gazette*. That's fine by me. But you got to give me something in return. So why don't you start by telling me about what went on between you and Zeke? When I know your angle I can save you a lot of trouble by helping you to find whatever it is you're looking for.'

Harker thought for a moment, then said: 'Fair enough,' and proceeded to give a plain, unvarnished account of the events of Mason Canyon.

Abe listened carefully, then plied Harker with questions to establish that Harker had not provoked Zeke in any way, had not shot him, and had acted like a good citizen by bringing the body to Laureston instead of leaving it on the trail. But Harker was less forthcoming about his own history and background and his reasons for being in the area.

'But I'll tell you some of it and about why I'm here,' he said. 'In the War, I had a buddy. A good man. Name of Billy Boden. Know him?'

Abe thought a moment.

'Name's familiar. Got it! Staked himself a claim up in Bluestone Valley a few years back, part of that Government land scheme. There was some trouble. I forget the details but I wrote it up at the time. We'll dig out the back numbers in a while. Meanwhile, carry on.'

'When the War was over, he decided to come out west and settle down. He was married by then. He couldn't see life for a family working out in Illinois. Last he told me he was heading out this way. I stayed on in the army for a spell. But the peacetime routine got too much for me. I got my discharge two years ago. Since then, I been lots of places and done all kind of jobs, but that's neither here nor there. One day, in a bar in St Louis, I thought of my old army pal, Billy Boden, and I decided to look him up. I headed out this way, not knowing exactly where he'd put roots down or even if he was still of a mind to. I asked after him along the trail and finally I've caught up with him in this fine town of Laureston. And then, on the way, some kid I never heard of took a shot at me.'

'And you ain't the first. No, sir. There's been four or five shootings in Mason Canyon in the last two months. All done the same way. Single rider, shot in the head, no robbery, no reason for it, no witnesses. So unless there's someone wants to deny the obvious, I guess we found the shooter: Zeke Viall.'

'You going to print that?'

'Not this week,' said Abe, shaking his head, 'and maybe not next. I'll report what happened to you but I'll wait for what Judge Morton has to say in court about the rest of it. I don't dare come straight and say what any man of sense would see at once, because it would not only be an unsubstantiated allegation for which I could be closed down, but Walter Viall, who draws a lot of water round here, would send in half a dozen irate readers in his employ and smash the press I got in my back room.'

'As bad as that?' asked Harker, raising one eyebrow.

'Every bit,' said Abe.

Harker frowned. He'd heard of places like Laureston. All quiet and orderly on the surface. But underneath, too many people going in fear for their families, their property, their livelihoods and even their lives.

'Let's go see how Billy Boden's been doing,' he said.

Abe showed him through the back

room, past the hand press and out into a yard where he kept the files in a dusty lean-to wooden cabin. He unlocked the door, lit a lamp and for a couple of hours, even after the raucous shouts of the hotel's last customers had died away, they pored over the old news.

By the time they were done, Harker had fleshed out the bare bones of the story Sheriff Rukatch had told him.

The settlers who'd arrived about the same time as Billy Boden had all been forced out. Judge Morton had rejected their claim that they'd been prevented by persons unknown from working their land, ruled that they had 'decided' of their own free will to be indolent, and that their claims and any buildings on them should be confiscated and sold by auction. Harker was not surprised to see the name of Walter Viall appear as the new owner of all the dozen properties bar one.

'If you think he got them cheap, you'd be right,' said Abe. 'It was so obvious. He scared off all genuinely interested buyers who stayed away, paid stooges to put in low bids and then drop out pretty quick, leaving all the lots to come to him at knock-down prices. Look and learn: that's how men get rich.'

Of the dispossessed settlers, three — Jake Stone, Dick Pipes, and Lovell Jackson — had stayed on, working ranges which they'd staked and worked for themselves. They now had to pay Viall rent for the privilege of doing the same job for him.

The one settler Viall hadn't driven out was Billy Boden. Even so, Billy had complained publicly that strong-arm tactics had been used against him, his family and his property. When his wife had come into Laureston, to go to church or visit the store, she'd been jostled and jeered and the traces of her buggy had been cut. There were never any witnesses to the treatment she'd got and nothing was done to prevent it. So she'd stopped coming to town and on the rare occasions when Billy came he finished his business as fast as he could before news got around that he was there.

But even Billy didn't come in any more.

Viall had gone on harassing him. Billy, being one against many, was in no position to defend himself. In time his herd declined and ceased to be a viable proposition. So he set up as a miller. He built a mill and put the word around that the arable farmers didn't need to pay to use the mill on Viall's spread out of town or cart their corn forty miles to be ground at Acre Creek because there was a new mill they could use only a short step from the centre of Laureston.

It never happened.

There was no trouble before the mill was finished. Then a gang of whooping, drunken, unidentified riders arrived one night and burnt it to the ground.

Next, Billy built a still. As soon as it was ready, it was raided by masked men who smashed it. That was just under a year ago. Billy hadn't come up with any new ideas since, because he'd had a leg broken when he tried to defend the still. Abe reckoned it wasn't over yet.

'Why doesn't Viall just run him off the land?' asked Harker. 'What's holding him back?'

'I've often wondered that myself,' said Abe, 'but I never came up with an answer.'

'It's late,' said Harker, rising to his feet.

'Well?' said Abe eagerly. 'What d'you make of it? What you going to do?'

'First thing,' said Harker, 'is to get some shut eye. I get tired on days when people fire guns at me and try to shoot my head off my shoulders. Then tomorrow, I'll head out Bluewater Valley way, meet up with old Billyboy and have me a look-see. Thanks for all the help.'

As he turned to leave, Abe said:

'Listen, Harker. Viall may be a bad man but this ain't a bad town. There's good people have come here over the years and what they've made is worth saving. If there's anything I can do to help, you be sure and let me know, because I want to see Walt Viall stopped. I want Laureston cleaned up.'

'Sure, Abe. When something happens, you'll be the first to know.'

Leaving Abe to lock up, Harker left the offices of the *Laureston Gazette* and headed back down the street towards the hotel.

It was very late and Laureston was asleep. A fitful moon whitened roofs and picked out the white lines of the boardwalks before slipping behind a cloud and plunging the night into blackness again. The air was still warm and it moved slowly against Harker's face. It brought him the scent of tobacco.

He stiffened and put his hand to the gun in his holster.

The moon, throwing off a scudding scarf of cloud, suddenly showed the empty street and revealed a darker patch of shadow against the white-painted front of Sam Whipple's grocery store away to Harker's left. The shadow moved.

31

Harker abandoned the middle of the road and ran for cover in a side street. Now his gun was in his hand. He looked carefully round the corner of the first building in the street. He was just in time to see that the dark patch had gone before the moon wrapped itself once more in cloud and covered the town in darkness. Emerging from his hiding place, he crossed the street at a crouching run and stooped to take stock behind a wagon parked outside the livery stables where he'd left his horse. He waited.

In the next quarter of an hour, occasional rustlings, whispering and sudden bursts of moonlight left him pretty certain that there were three men not in bed and up to no good on the streets of Laureston. He was willing to bet a bundle that each of them had a gun and were all on Walt Viall's payroll. They were getting restless, running out of patience.

One was stationed twenty yards to his left, to cut him off if he went that way.

Another was on a roof opposite, well hidden, a sniper, with a view over the entrance to the hotel. Harker had had a bellyful of snipers for one day. A third had taken up a position in an alley across the way from the hotel, thirty yards further down the street. Waiting until a cloud turned the moonlight off, Harker stepped into the road, where his boots made no noise in the dust, and moved quickly towards the first man. He circled round the back of the buildings fronting the main street and re-emerged some twenty yards further along. Harker's fix on the man's position was confirmed by a weak shaft of moonlight which showed not only his hat and checked shirt but the gun he held in his fist. Slowly, deliberately, Harker worked his way up behind him. The man never knew what hit him. It might as well have been a falling tree as the butt of a Colt, for the result was the same. He went down without making a sound.

Harker picked up his gun and threw

it into the shadows behind him. Then he switched his attention to the gunman in the alley opposite the hotel twenty yards down the street.

A horse snorted in its sleep just across the street. It was still hitched to a flatbed wagon. From the back of the wagon came the sound of snoring. Harker smiled. Some roisterer who'd taken a drop too much to drink in the hotel bar had decided he wouldn't make it home and, seeing as how the night was warm, was spending it sleeping off the drink he had taken.

Harker untied the reins from the hitching rail, led the rig into the middle of the street and got up into the driving seat. When the horse was fully awake, he reached forward and thwacked it on the rump with the whip. Startled, it set off at a gallop, crashing through the night and shattering the silence. Harker steered it to the side of the street, waited until the rig was almost level with the alley, and jumped feet first.

His boots caught the waiting man in

the chest and knocked him off his feet. Harker was on him at once, straddling him before sending him to the land where the lights are always out with a hard right on the jaw. Two down, one to go.

But number three was a problem. He could be shot off his perch easy. But that would bring people running: the Sheriff asking questions, townsfolk wondering who was this newcomer who brought dead bodies with him and made more the moment he arrived, and not least Viall. He wasn't ready yet for Viall.

The horse and rig were still filling the night with their noise. Making the most of the distraction and a thicket of lunar shadow, Harker ran quickly across the street and was inside the hotel before the moon came out again. When he closed the door behind him, the street was silent again.

The night man looked up from the paper he was reading.

'You got a visitor,' the man said,

looking at him with a certain respect. Harker couldn't say why the man looked at him that way.

'What sort of visitor?'

'Waiting for you. Upstairs.'

'Can I get a drink here?' he said.

The night man reached one hand down to a shelf under his counter and produced a bottle of whisky and two glasses.

Harker took the bottle and the glasses, turned and made for the stairs.

'Thanks,' he said to the disappointed night man who'd been hoping to get a taste in one of the glasses of what was in the bottle. 'Put it on the bill.'

To the right of the reception desk was a staircase with a red carpet on it. Harker took the stairs two at a time. When he reached the top, he paused. The silence inside the hotel was as thick as it was out in the street but it wasn't as dark. Glims flickering on the walls at intervals showed the lines of the corridor and the doors of all ten of the hotel's rooms. Not many people came to Laureston, which had a stage-coach depot but no railway, the nearest being fifty rugged miles north, and folks who did come never stopped many nights.

Even from the top of the stairs, he could see that the door to his room at the end of the corridor was open. A bar of light lay across the floor. Treading softly for so big a man, Harker moved cautiously down the corridor, shifting the bottle and the glasses to his left hand as he went and taking the Colt from the holster at his hip with his right.

He kicked the door wide open and was inside as quick as a fox, eyes everywhere and gun up. Then he relaxed.

Sitting in a chair next to the window was the handsomest woman he had seen since he was in St Louis. A lady. Not yet thirty. Even complexion. Small waist. A dress like ladies go to balls in, poise like ladies preside over the tea-table with, and a look in her eye that said it would take two earthquakes and a flood to unsettle her ladylike composure. Of the two, Harker was the most surprised.

'Put your gun up, sit down, pour us a drink apiece,' she said coolly, 'and then tell me what you want with Billy Boden.'

Harker obeyed the first three of these commands, handed the lady her drink and raised his glass to her.

'Your health, Miss — ?'

'Missus. Mrs Strafford. Your good health, Mr Harker.'

'And what can I do for you, ma'am?'

'I heard you've been asking after Billy Boden. Is it true you were with him in the army?'

'True as true. Served by his side two years and four months. But where did you hear about that?'

'I own this hotel, Mr Harker. A person in my position gets to hear a lot of things. I also heard you spent the evening with Abe Monkman. It's now very late. I've been asking myself what you two boys could have had so much to talk about? You've kept a lady waiting, Mr Harker. It's not considered a polite thing to do.'

'My apologies, ma'am, but I had a few problems getting back. Made me later than I planned.'

'I've been watching by the window. Women who wait are supposed to watch out of windows.'

'And what did you see out the window?'

'I saw how you handle yourself. You are a resourceful man, Mr Harker.'

Tom Harker leaned back in his chair and looked into her eyes.

'And now tell me about yourself, Mrs Strafford,' he said. 'It would only be polite.'

'I'll tell you when you've told me what exactly you want with Billy Boden.'

'Very well, it's no secret. Billy left the service before me and since I got my discharge I've been knocking about, trying this and that here and there, and generally getting nowhere. Billy told me he was thinking of settling down. He mentioned several places including this neck of the woods. I tried all the others. Said he was interested in the Government's scheme for encouraging people to settle on Indian territory in this part of the west and open it up. Wherever I went I'd ask for him and finally I seem to have caught up with him here in Laureston. I'm planning on going up to Bluewater Valley in the morning. I hear he ain't doing so good. That's it. End of story. Now it's your turn, Mrs Strafford.'

'I'm Billy's sister. I'm Tabitha.'

Harker stared. Yes, there was no doubt about it. The directness of the gaze, the straightforwardness of the manner, the humour lurking at the corner of her mouth.

'Now I know, I can see the family resemblance. Except — '

'Except?' said Tabitha.

'Except he ain't nowhere as pretty as you!' he said with a grin.

The pink glow that suddenly appeared

on her cheek might have been a blush. When she spoke, he knew it was anger.

'Don't play fool games, Mr Harker. There's no time for it. How long do you think it'll be before Viall finds out you're here and sends a dozen of his men to snuff you out for doing what you did to Zeke? Now listen to me.'

She leaned forward in her chair. Her eyes were cold.

'Stay away from Billy! He's in enough of a jam already without you drawing Walt Viall's thugs after him. Walt and me, well, we've got a sort of under-standing.'

'What sort of understanding?'

'That's no business of yours. I've gone as far as I'm going with you by telling you who I am. Look, Mr Harker, Billy needs to be protected from a very powerful man. I found a way of doing it. I keep Walt away from Billy and Billy doesn't go looking for trouble. As long as he keeps out of Walt Viall's way, he's in no danger. Result: the situation is in hand. I won't have anyone endangering the fine balance I've managed to create. So I'm telling you, not asking you, if you are really a good friend of Billy's, leave town tonight. And don't come back.'

Harker stared at her.

'Way I hear it, this fine balance ain't doing Billy a lot of good, him having his mill and his still wrecked, his leg broke and his wife too frightened to come into town.'

'Go!' said Tabitha Strafford as she stood up. 'I won't stay to argue. I can't afford to be seen talking to you. I don't want to be found here when Viall's men show up.'

Harker tried to stop her but she swept regally from the room and was gone.

Harker poured himself another drink. How did this Tabitha keep the peace between her brother and a bull like Viall?

He doused the light and took a look out of the window to check the street. He caught a movement and looked again. Half a dozen men had gathered in the alley across the way. Harker knew they weren't there for a prayer meeting. Nobody takes guns to church and those boys had guns. At least one each.

3

Bluewater Valley

Harker wasn't a man to duck a fight but he decided to sit this one out. It wasn't that he didn't like the odds. But he had no idea what he had got into in Laureston. He wasn't going to start shooting back and dig himself in any deeper until he knew what it was all about.

He decided to make himself scarce, go see Billy, figure out what in tarnation was going on.

The stables would be locked up snug this time of night. There was no way he'd get his horse out now. Stealing one wasn't a good idea. In country where a man couldn't get far without something to ride, nobody likes a horse thief.

Swallowing the last of his drink, he let himself out of his room and made for the end of the corridor. He pulled up the sash of the window which looked out over a side street, swung one leg over the sill and let himself fall. He landed on all fours, quiet as fog. He turned left, away from the main street. When he was clear of the last buildings, he made slanting, crouching runs for every piece of available cover. It was beginning to get light and he didn't want to be caught in open country on foot.

He took a bearing by the stars and the cross on the church roof and plotted a rough course to the Blue Mountains which Sheriff Rukatch had pointed out to him. Their tops had just started to glow dawn pink.

Harker didn't lope like a mountain man nor stride like a plainsman. He was a horseman and swung his hips as he walked into the new day. From time to time he turned and looked back the way he'd come. He saw no one and the further he went the more relaxed he became.

The country rose slowly through wooded slopes and gentle valleys. When he reached the foot of the hills, the valleys grew deeper, the streams flowed faster and the branches of the trees dipped down until they almost touched the rushing water. Harker was about to stop and take a drink when he heard a shout.

He turned and saw a posse of maybe a dozen riders heading fast his way. Had they seen him? He didn't wait to find out but broke into his crouching run. He made for the nearest valley. It was broad here but would get steeper and narrower the further he went. Maybe it was a dead-end. But for the moment the trees which grew on its lush slopes offered good cover. He heard another shout. It was closer. This time he knew he'd been spotted.

He began to run faster. He moved up that valley at a good speed. A narrow trail bordering the stream, less a trail and more an animal run, made the going easy. But if it was easy for him it was also easy for his pursuers who began gaining on him fast. If he didn't get out of sight soon, they'd run him down.

The trail had been more or less straight so far. Suddenly it took a detour round a large rock barring its path. The rock was maybe fifteen feet high and had its back half buried in the steep valley side. Behind him and gaining fast, Harker heard the front rider crashing through the undergrowth lining the trail. Time to get out of sight, take to rougher ground, rob the men chasing him of speed, of the advantage they had over him. And then a thought struck him.

Maybe he could borrow a horse.

He stopped in his tracks. With his breath rasping deep in his chest, he stood and examined the boulder. Towering above him, he looked down the length of its worn, smooth sandstone façade. He ran round back of it, skipping off the trail through low bushes, and inspected the boulder again. From here he could see enough cracks and crannies to give him decent hand- and foot-holds. He began to climb. When he got to the top, he peered down on the trail and steadied himself.

The sound of the approaching rider got louder. Soon, to judge by the rate he was going, he would burst out of a grove of low bushes not more than ten yards distant. The moment that happened, he'd have Harker in full view. But by that time it would be too late to stop or draw a gun. Harker stood up, controlled his breathing, and waited for his chance.

One moment the bushes were swaying innocently in the breeze. The next, they parted angrily as a horse and rider brushed them aside. The man looked up, saw Harker, reined back his horse. But his momentum carried him forward and his hand was nowhere near his gun when Harker jumped him and wrestled him to the ground.

The impact separated them and left

both men momentarily winded. The rider was first to react. He staggered to his feet, bore down on Harker and aimed a kick at his head. Harker saw it coming, grabbed his boot and twisted it hard. His attacker lost his balance and crashed to the ground. It was all Harker needed. He was on his man instantly and knocked him cold with a right to the temple followed by a heavy left to the jaw.

He looked up only to see the rump of his pursuer's horse disappear along the trail. Startled at being jumped, it had bolted. Harker swore. He heard the sound of its hoofs pummelling the trail twenty, thirty yards away, growing fainter.

Then he was up and running again. He quickly lost the sound of the horse up ahead and became aware of other riders at his back, gaining on him. He heard a shout: they had found the man Harker had put out of the game. For a moment, there was a lull and Harker made ground on them. But then he heard more shouts and on they came.

Harker was now racing along a level stretch of the river bank. There was no way he could keep up this pace. He was beginning to feel winded. He ran another fifty yards through the willows on the bank, then splashed into the tumbling stream, hoping to find a patch of reeds or a fallen tree to hide him. Here the stream slowed, widened and fanned out into a broad pool. He saw the log jam responsible for slowing the stream and turning it into a small lake. A beaver lodge rose about 10 feet above the surface of the water, which was about the same depth. Diving under the water he surfaced inside the beaver house, which was made on two storeys and was big enough to accommodate several men. Harker hauled himself out of the water and found a dry, comfortable resting place on the upper level of the structure. He tried to quiet his breathing. He heard his pursuers arrive but could see nothing of them, how many they were, what sort of men they were. But they stopped. Voices came to him. They'd spotted the snapped twigs and his tracks in the grass where he'd left the trail. They dismounted and beat the undergrowth in their attempts to find him. They even stood on the roof of the beaver house. For a moment Harker expected to hear them breaking it open. Maybe they'd set it on fire to smoke him out. There was more confused shouting, then silence. He waited. Then he waited some more.

He heard only the gurgle of water. As he relaxed, he was aware of its hypnotic effect and, having missed a night in a hotel bed, he was soon asleep.

He woke several hours later. He listened for anything that might betray the presence of his pursuers but heard nothing. He slid off his shelf into the water, swam out of the beaver house and very carefully broke the surface of the water, ready to submerge again at the first sign of danger.

But the banks of the stream were

deserted and, warily but with growing confidence, Harker scrambled back to solid ground.

He dried and checked his Colt then started back down the valley, intending to pick up his route to Bluewater. He grew cautious again as he approached the boulder where he had jumped his man. But the place was deserted and he did not linger. The sun was still hot enough to dry off the rest of his clothes as he walked.

When he got to the mouth of the valley, he paused in the cover of a cottonwood tree and looked long and hard at the plain which stretched away before him. He saw cattle in small groups grazing, but no sign of riders. Finally, he stepped out into the open.

No one shot at him. He went on his way.

Within a mile, the trail began to climb steeply. It took him up onto another ledge of land. There were more cattle here, for the grass was green and lush. He was surprised. From what he'd been told, Billy had lost most of his herd one way or another. Curious, he stepped off the trail and headed slowly towards a couple of head which had detached themselves from the main herd. They looked up as he approached, stopped chewing, swished their tails then walked away unhurriedly. As they went, he saw that their hides were marked, not BB as he was expecting, but WV.

What were Walter Viall's cattle doing on Billy Boden's range?

Another half hour's walking brought him within sight of a homestead made of heavy timber. It had a garden, with a fence round it, and a barn. Smoke coiled up from the chimney. There was no other sign of life.

Even so, Harker approached cautiously. He was ten yards from the fence when the door opened. A woman stepped on to the porch. She was at the age when pretty turns to something deeper. She had auburn hair and was holding a shotgun. It was pointed at him.

'Who are you?' said the woman. 'What do you want?'

'Mrs Boden? I'm a friend of Billy's. We were in the army together. Is he about?'

'What's your name?'

'Harker. Tom Harker. Maybe Billy mentioned me?'

She paused a moment, then said: 'What do you know about Cedar Creek?'

Harker struggled a moment then remembered. It was in the last days of the War. He and Billy were in a unit that had held a hilltop against a hundred enemy troopers for half a day. When at last they were relieved, they dropped back behind their lines and rested up at a creek overhung with dark green cedars. As they were arriving, Billy, who was carrying a half dozen ammunition belts, most with fresh cartridges, slung over his shoulder, slipped on the muddy bank and fell into a deep pool. All the men laughed. But when he didn't resurface, Harker

54

realized the weight of the belts was holding him down. He dived in, pulled him out, and dragged him onto dry land. When he'd stopped coughing water, Billy calmly reached inside his open tunic and produced a still wriggling fish and said: 'Supper!' which had made everyone break up.

'Cedar Creek?' said Harker. 'Fish for supper!'

'That'll do it,' said the woman with a half smile. 'He loves telling that story. Come on in.'

She lowered the gun, propped it against the wall by the door and stepped back into the house. Harker followed. Once inside, he saw plain furniture and neatness.

'Is Billy home, Mrs Boden?'

'Call me Martha, then I'll call you Tom. No, he's not home. I can't rightly say where he is. I hope he's still in town. I'm scared for him.'

'But I heard he never went to Laureston any more.'

'Who told you that?'

'Tabitha.'

'You met Tabitha?'

She sounded surprised.

'If Tabitha told you that,' she said, 'she'll have told you Billy don't exactly see eye to eye with our local cattle baron. He's not here because Walter Viall sent men to fetch him to town. Something's changed. It don't feel the same as it did, Tom. I'm sick with worry. But what am I thinking of,' she said. 'Let me fix you some coffee. Billy'd not forgive me if I didn't.'

While he drank his coffee, Martha filled in the details. A dozen of Viall's men had hauled him out of the house, said their boss wanted to see him, sat him on a horse and then rode off with him.

'Did they say what it was about?'

'What it's always about,' said Martha bitterly. 'It's about Viall's plans to be cattle king of all the plains. Bluewater is the only range left that he doesn't own.'

'But as I came I saw Viall's cows everywhere.'

'That's how he operates. He's moved part of his herd on to our land. Then when we go to the law to defend ourselves, he'll say we didn't have any cows on it, that we weren't using the land for the purpose the government gave it to us for, so we're not entitled to stay on it. He wants us out, Tom. Always did. Until now, he's held off. I guess that was Tabitha's doing. But seems like something happened to change all that. That's the only reason I can think of to explain why Viall has made a move now.'

Harker thought a moment, then said:

'Has Tabitha got something on him? I know she comes over pretty forceful. But from what I hear, Viall isn't a man to let himself be railroaded easily.'

'We've asked her, but she won't say. But whatever it is, it's worked fine until today.'

Harker heard a baby cry. Martha got up, went into a back room and returned with a bundle in her arms.

'Meet Tom Boden,' she said with a

smile. 'Billy named him after you. I would have preferred Robert, but now I've met you, I like Tom fine. My husband's a good man. He deserves better than being pushed around by the likes of Viall. Here, hold him, while I make us a bite to eat.'

Harker took young Tom who looked up and smiled. Then Harker handed him back.

'I don't want to be ungrateful, ma'am, but I won't stay. It would be best all round if I went along to see what Viall wants with Billy. Do you have a horse I could borrow? I left town in a hurry,' he said with a rueful smile, 'before sun-up, before the stable was open. My mount is still back in Laureston.'

'Of course,' said Martha, 'but you can't go before you've eaten. I'll be quick.'

Later, she took him round to the stable at the back of the house. Harker saddled a roan and minutes later was riding back the way he'd come, with a woman's hopes still ringing in his ears.

The roan wasn't built for speed but it had stamina. Harker took it along at steady pace which ate the miles but wasn't so fast that he couldn't keep his eyes peeled for trouble.

He looked hard but didn't see any.

A couple of hours later he rode into Laureston and stopped by the sheriff's office.

'Didn't think I'd be seeing you again, son,' said Rukatch. 'They're saying you cracked a few heads here last night and Viall's men are mighty sore. Viall don't like it neither. He ain't used to having anyone stand up to him. What you aiming to do next? You'd better have a care. There's a dozen men with guns got it in for you. But if there's anything I can do to help, just say the word.'

'One simple thing you can do for me, Sheriff. Viall sent some of his boys out to Bluewater and hauled Billy Boden into town. Now, where would they take Billy so he and Viall could have a quiet chat?'

Rukatch scratched his head.

'Nothing comes to mind straight away. He's got a spread east of town. But if he's in Laureston, the place to start is the hotel. It's where he goes when he's in town.'

'Then that's where I'll start looking.'

4

First Blood

The bar in Tabitha Strafford's hotel was more narrow than wide, and deeper than it was broad. Along the length of its right-hand wall ran a fancy hardwood bar skirted by a brass foot-rail. A man leaning on the bar taking a drink could watch himself or the rest of the customers behind him in the mirrors which hung in gilt frames on the wall. Or he could study the painting of a wagon train moving across a wide plain like a fleet of sailing ships or, as the bar-room wits said, a flock of sheep being led to slaughter. The rest of the place was filled with tables and hard-backed chairs. Moose heads with impressive antlers were mounted on the walls from which sconces for candles projected at intervals. Halfway along

61

was a large oil chandelier, and oil-lamps hung from the ceiling at intervals. At the back, where it was dim even when it was broad day outside, some lamps were already lit. They showed the doors to three private rooms.

Harker pushed through the swing doors, looked around and walked up to the bar.

'You seen Walter Viall?' he said pleasantly.

Before the barkeep could reply, a voice at Harker's back said: 'Who's asking?'

Harker turned round slowly and found himself staring at a large man, though he was nowhere as tall as a fir-tree nor as wide as an ox-cart.

'Where's he at?' said Harker.

Instead of replying, the big man raised his right fist to about the level of his ear. Before he could release its power, a smaller fist uncoiled itself faster than a striking rattler and caught him in the throat. The big man's face froze, partly with pain and partly with the surprise of it, because no one had hit him so hard since his pa had larruped him when was in short pants. His raised fist dropped and clutched his windpipe, he began coughing and collapsed onto the floor where he writhed, struggling for breath.

Harker ignored him, turned back to the barkeep and raised an eyebrow.

'Through there, mister,' the man said nervously, pointing to a door at the back. 'Private party.'

'Much obliged,' said Harker and walked through the men sitting at tables. Not all had witnessed the demolition, for it had happened so fast, so those who had began telling the others what they had seen. But every last jack of them craned his neck to get a look at Big Elk Moses choking in the sawdust on the floor. It wasn't a sight you saw often. Big Moses was Viall's bodyguard, never bested. Until now. Nobody offered to help him.

Harker was in no mood for pleasantries. He had come to Laureston to look up an old army pal. He'd been shot at, men had tried to punch his head off and fill him full of holes. He didn't like it. He wasn't going to take it any more. Harker had started to get mad.

He flung open the door and took in the scene at a glance. Billy Boden was tied to one chair, an older man who he took to be Viall was sitting, arms folded and facing him, in another. Two brawny men were taking turns to reinforce their boss's questions with doses of physical persuasion. Billy's face was swollen, a mass of blood. As the door opened, the two men looked up and Viall turned in his chair, frowning, not liking it that he'd been disturbed.

Without breaking his stride, Harker marched up to him.

'You're Viall?'

'And you're the man who killed my boy.'

'I killed nobody, but he was trying to kill me. Did you send him out to Mason Canyon to gun down me in particular or was it his idea to take a pop at whoever came along, for practice, for fun, whatever?'

'Jimmy, Ben, get this man out of here,' was Viall's answer.

'Sure thing, Mr Viall,' said Jimmy, a stocky, small-eyed bruiser who weighed maybe a hundred and fifty pounds and looked as if he kept himself in condition.

'No problem,' said the other. Ben was taller, bigger, dark, maybe twenty-five.

Harker was in no mood to be fooled with. But this wasn't a shooting situation, nobody need get killed here. He wasn't against the idea, but bullets would complicate things. The main business was to get Billy away. Then they could put their heads together and work out what to do, long term, about Viall.

Viall! What made a man like that think he could land on a decent, hard-working town and rearrange it to suit himself? What sort of country were they building out here in the West if any thug with a fancy to be a big boss could just muscle in, ride roughshod over the rule of law, tell people to do what he said just because he had money and could pay men to make folk dance to his tune? That's how the Old World of kings and lords had worked. The New World of the West wasn't going to make the same mistake if Harker had anything to do with it. Anyway, there was one thing he hated, and that was a bully. It made him real mad. Standing looking down at Viall, he saw a bully. Harker felt himself getting madder by the minute.

'Leave him to me, Mr Viall, sir,' grinned Jimmy and he lunged at Harker.

Harker leaned back a couple of inches, putting his chin beyond the range of Jimmy's fists.

'Put them up, sonny,' he said. 'I don't want to hurt you.'

Jimmy paused in mid swing. Sonny! This dude was going to get the beating of his life. He came forward again. He didn't get very far.

Harker got under his guard with a vicious short right that caught him flush on the bottom edge of his rib cage. Jimmy felt something give, he might even have heard a crack and then he was down, rolling on the floor in agony, nursing a couple of broken ribs, gasping for breath.

Viall stared down at him and snarled: 'Get up! I told you to get this man out of here! It's what I pay you for!'

'It's OK, Mr Viall, I can take him.' said Ben.

'So do it!' snapped Viall.

Harker stepped back, to give himself room. But he didn't need it. Ben squared up, like the more 'scientific' kind of fighter. He dodged and ducked and bobbed and weaved. He poked out a left and followed up with a right, but all he hit was air. Then Harker stepped in. He felt his anger boil over, and he didn't try to control it any more. A crashing left split Ben's cheek to the bone and a right flattened his nose. Harker felt the soft crunch of gristle as both nostrils collapsed and the sensation made him madder. These men who came from nowhere were like foxes that get into a chicken coop. They didn't just take what they needed, they killed and maimed and wrecked whatever came to hand, for the pleasure of being strong. Harker had seen enough of such men to know that if there weren't any troublemaking foxes, there'd be no need for sheriffs and marshals to look after the decent, honest folks. He put all his hatred for the breed into a series of body shots which drove all the breath out of Ben and brought his head swooping down to meet the uppercut which started from somewhere around Harker's right knee. Ben's head snapped back, his eyes glassed over and he would have gone down if a combination of right and left hadn't held him up on his feet by their sheer power. The fists went on coming at him even after he stopped being aware of them, driving him back, keeping him upright so he could take more, blood pouring out of him, helpless.

Suddenly Harker was aware of a bleeding face in front of him, of two eyes staring at him vacantly, of two arms dangling limply. His fury subsided and he took a step back. He saw Ben hang there for a moment, topple slowly to his left and crash to the floor at Viall's feet. He lay still. He didn't even moan.

In the room, silence hung like a palpable presence. The men crowding round the door looked on, awed into silence by the savagery they had just seen unleashed. Viall hadn't moved out of his chair. It was Harker, unmarked and hardly breathing faster than normal, who broke the silence. He grabbed Viall by the lapels of his jacket and hauled him to his feet as if he were a rag doll, though he was not a small man.

'Your boys couldn't put me out, so how's about you giving it a whirl. You're the big man around here. You're always giving orders. Now see if you can do what you get your boys to do for you. You got the stomach for it? You going to do your own dirty work for once?'

Viall, chin hunched in the collar of his shirt, with Harker's fingers an inch from his neck, felt fear. He'd never seen such savage beatings handed out with such controlled fury. He'd been afraid in the War. Who hadn't? He'd been afraid when there were Indians on his tail. But then the enemy had been distant and there was action he could take. Now, he was here, facing six feet of icy, focused, steely menace, and there was nothing he could do.

Then Harker relaxed. The ferocity faded from his expression. He released Viall who fell back down heavily in his chair. But he wasn't finished with him yet.

'Untie Billy,' said Harker, 'and don't be rough.'

Aware of the eyes watching from the doorway, humiliated as he had never been in all his life, Viall fumbled with the ropes that held Billy.

Harker helped his friend to his feet.

'Hello, pardner' he said. 'It's been a long time.'

'What kept you?' said Billy attempting a grin that made him wince.

Harker, taking Billy's arm and looping it over his shoulder, helped him towards the door. The men who had watched the scene moved back to make way. As they cleared the door Harker called out, without turning round:

'This ain't over yet, Viall. You and me both will finish our business some other time. Don't go away. I'll be back.'

He heard the door slam behind him.

He sat Billy in a chair, sent word to fetch a doctor and ordered whiskey. Billy drank some of it and spilled the rest down the front of his shirt. His mouth had been temporarily rearranged and wasn't much use for drinking purposes or for talking or laughing.

Doc Prentice came, patched Billy up

and helped with the whiskey. He didn't spill any of it.

'Could be worse. Lot of bruising, nothing broken except teeth. Keep him quiet and he'll be fine.'

'I'll get him home. But he's not up to riding. Where can I get a buggy or a buckboard?'

'Use mine,' said Doc Prentice. 'I'll drive. We'll take the rest of the bottle with us. Whiskey has medicinal properties. It's a scientific fact: it's the ideal drink for a doctor.'

He took another snort before getting up.

'I'd best go and see to the wounded in the back room. Viall will doubtless be out hollering for me any minute now. Don't want to do it. Rather not do it. Don't like Viall, don't like his boys. But doctors tend the sick. It's what doctors do. There are sick men in that room and I'm a doctor. So I go.'

As he went, he called for a bottle of whiskey from the barman.

'Charge it to Mr Viall, son. It's

medicine, I'm prescribing it for his stricken employees.'

Suddenly a voice at Harker's back said: 'What's going on here?'

Harker turned and saw Tabitha Strafford.

'Was just passing, ma'am. Thought I'd sit in on the business meeting I heard Walt Viall was having with your brother. Seems I arrived just in time to stop them falling out big time. Boys will be boys.'

He stared so hard at her that she flinched. She averted her eyes and took a closer look at the broken figure slumped in a chair bleeding on the floor of her hotel. She gave a start when she recognized the man under the mess.

'Billy? Is that you? My God, what happened?'

'Let Tom tell it,' Billy muttered through cracked lips.

'Well?' said Tabitha, turning to Harker.

'Seems your friend Viall sent some of his toughs out to Bluewater to fetch

Billy in for a chat. I guess he didn't like what Billy had to say or got impatient when he didn't say anything at all. You know as well as I do how stubborn he can be.'

'Where's Walt now?'

'He's in the back room, with a couple of his men. They ain't feeling well. They sort of fell over.'

The men listening laughed.

Tabitha's eyes narrowed.

'Did Walt fall over too?' she asked.

'Nope. He just slipped off his high horse for a moment. But he's fine,' said Harker. 'So far,' added Harker, at a loss to read her thoughts.

'This isn't the way,' she said and, turning on her heel, she made for the back room. Harker was left to work out what she meant by those parting words. Wondering which side she was on, he didn't wait for her to reappear but got Billy to his feet and walked him through the swing doors and out onto the boardwalk where Sheriff Rukatch had just arrived.

'Looks like I missed all the action,' he said. 'Want to tell me what it was about?'

'Nothing to tell, Sheriff.'

'But this man looks badly hurt.'

'Just a conversation that got a little heated. It's over. Just a few bruises is all.'

'That's right, Silas,' said a voice in the crowd. 'That and an exhibition of the pugilist's noble art.'

The drinkers from the saloon raised a guffaw.

'This ain't the place,' said Rukatch. 'We'll talk later. You can fill me in.'

'Careful, Silas,' said the same voice, 'he don't need no encouragement. He's a good hand at filling people in!'

This witticism brought another laugh. Rukatch gave up.

The doc came out through the swing doors.

'What the hell did you hit those men with?' he said quietly to Harker. 'They'll get over it, but not for a while. I patched them up but the whiskey will do more good than I can. They'll need time. Come on, let's go, before Viall gets over the shock.'

The old timer he'd sent to harness his buckboard appeared on cue. They loaded Billy on to the back of it. While this was going on, Harker retrieved his horse from the livery stable and hitched both it and the horse he'd borrowed from Martha Boden to the back of the buckboard. He climbed up next to Doc Prentice who flicked the reins over the draw horse's back.

As they disappeared round the end of the street, the crowd of men went back into the hotel. There was enough to talk about to last the old ones a lifetime and the young ones would be telling their grandchildren about it in forty years time.

On the trail, Harker asked:

'Who is Walter Viall? He been in these parts long?'

'Arrived a few years back, not long after the War ended. Started small but always talked and acted big. Brought a couple of hundred steers with him. But then he bought up Old Man Tuckerby's place out on the Santa Fe road, with all the stock. Got it cheap, they say, a bit of a question mark over the purchase. Then he just got bigger. More cows, more acres, more men to look after the acres and the cows.'

'All legit and above board?'

'There ain't nothing anyone could ever pin on him. But he uses methods that sail pretty close to the wind.'

'Like forcing the resale of government-lease land?'

'That sort of thing.'

'And buying judges?'

'Whole jurisdictions. Viall is making a name for himself in the county. He's got friends in high places. The word is he's got political ambitions.'

'Wouldn't surprise me none. He can only go so far in a place like Laureston. It's too small for him. But isn't there anyone in town prepared to stand up to him?'

'Silas Rukatch is a good man, but

he's on his own. There's also Abe Monkman who runs the *Gazette*. He speaks his mind as much as is wise in the circumstances. And there's ten or twelve men who got bounced off the government land claims they worked. Newt Thornton, Charlie Harris, José Bodega, among others. They're pretty sore. Maybe I've left a few out but I'd say there's a dozen handy men who're waiting for half a chance to put a spoke in Viall's wheel. But the rest of the townspeople either owe him favours or, like the storekeepers, liverymen and suppliers, can't afford to get on the wrong side of their biggest customer, however much they'd like to. All in all, opinion is against Walter Viall. But he's got a firm grip on the tender parts of the town's anatomy. So it's no surprise if he gets its silence and cooperation when he puts the squeeze on.'

Harker stopped asking questions and sat thinking while the buckboard's wheels turned. The level of whiskey in the bottle went down. So did the sun. It was between dog and wolf, as they say, when they got to Billy's place.

Martha didn't fuss, didn't throw a fit, didn't ask a lot of tomfool women's questions. She got a couch ready with a rug and cushions and Billy, who was feeling a touch stronger, stretched out on it. He even got outside of some of the beef stew that had been simmering on the stove all afternoon. Harker put much more of it away, for he'd been having a busy time. Doc Prentice kept to his whiskey diet. The quantity he transferred from bottle to gullet seemed to have no effect on him at all.

After supper, Harker got out the makings and rolled a cigarette for himself and Billy. The doc said no thanks — 'one vice at a time is my motto' — but he did say yes to a cup of coffee. As he sipped it, he said:

'Where do we go from here? You really mean to go back and finish it like you said?'

'All depends on Billy,' said Harker. 'It's his call. He's got a home here and a family in it. He picked a fine spot: good grazing, good water, good position not too far from Laureston. There's nothing says a man who's ready to roll up his sleeves couldn't make a go of it. But Viall is a powerful man and a nasty enemy to have. He's moved in on the claims of a dozen good men and pushed them out. And he'd have done the same to you, Billy, if it hadn't been for your sis. She told me she's been holding him back. She didn't say how. But looks like that don't work anymore. Viall has run his beef into Bluewater Valley and moved yours out. He'll have rebranded them WV by now, which means you've got nothing left, Billy. You're broke. You want to stay and fight or cut and run? A man with a family has to think carefully about these things.'

Billy started to open his mouth but it was Martha who answered.

'Of course he's staying. We haven't come this far and put so much work building the place up only to hand it over to scum like Viall and say: 'Here you are, kind sir, take everything we've got, and thanks very much for letting us go while we're still in one piece'.'

Doc Prentice whistled: 'If Viall has got Martha riled, then I don't give much for his chances. I feel sorry for him. What about you, Tom?'

'I'm in. I ain't shot anybody this week and I need the exercise. A run out against a soon-to-be ex-cattle king will fit the bill nicely.'

'You can count on me, too,' said the Doc. 'So what do we do?'

'Seems to me there's been too much sitting around waiting for Viall to make his next move. So we'll take the fight to him. We go on the offensive.'

'Can't fault the theory,' said the Doc. 'When do we start?'

'Now! Tonight!' said Harker.

5

Offensive

Harker went alone. There was no choice. Billy was out of it for now, and would be for a couple of days, and Doc Prentice was no gunsmith or raider, especially not after all the whiskey he'd put away. Harker had no grouse with that. He liked being on his own. If things went wrong, he'd have only himself to blame.

He hit the trail back towards Laureston. He was getting to know it well. Sheriff Rukatch had said Viall's spread was east of Laureston. So about a mile short of town, Harker turned off the trail and eventually picked up another, which led east, the Santa Fe road. After a couple of miles, he came to a stretch of road lined on each side by a rail fence. Then he came to a wooden sign with the WV brand on it and Viall's name underneath. A track ran off the road for half a mile before stopping at a cluster of buildings made up of a two-storey residence, bunkhouse, cook-shack and barns. There were no lights showing. Harker reined in and took stock. It was now around two in the morning.

It was another moonlit night and there was no wind. Apart from a few dry animal scutterings in the grass and the willows and cottonwoods at his back, the world was silent. There were cattle on the ranges to his left and right. They were asleep standing up and lying down. The fence lining the approach to the ranch was a picket-and-palissade affair, painted white, for effect. The rest of the fencing was less fancy and more workaday: a simple unpainted rail supported at intervals by wooden stakes.

Harker hid his horse among the trees, vaulted the fence and walked through the sleeping cows. He passed the ranch on his left and continued for another half mile up a slope which took him onto a wide plateau above and behind the ranch. In the distance, he saw successive folds in the land which turned into the foothills of the Blue Mountains rising majestic and snow-capped in the distance. Between him and the first foothill, in the middle of the plateau, was a lake. On the edge of the lake was a mill.

He investigated. It was a cornmill. It stood on the banks of the lake's main outlet. There was one set of sluices to shut off or open the supply to the millrace and another set to control the outflow of the lake itself. These second, much larger gates interested him most. They channelled the run-off into a valley. He followed its course down the slope until he reached a shallow basin, a man-made, artificial dam built of rocks and felled logs. The basin was used as a drinking hole for the WV ranch cattle. It was half full. Water in the basin flowed out from under the rocks and timber and ran down past the back of Viall's ranch. Input and output were carefully regulated to maintain the level of the water in the dam at a more or less steady depth. The proximity of a lake that size and the convenience of a constantly running, controllable stream made the site perfect for running cattle on. It also gave Harker an idea. He climbed back up to the lake.

Although the harvest was nowhere near ready to be gathered in and there was no corn to grind, the sluicegates had been kept well oiled. The same was true of the much heavier outflow sluices which controlled the level in the lower basin. They were three-quarters lowered. Harker did not need to strain any muscles raising them as high as they would go. The flow increased and soon the volume of water going with gravity thundered like a hundred buffalo fording a stream. Harker was not bothered by the noise. There was no one about to hear it except him.

He headed back down to the basin.

The water in it was already rising. He walked on. When he was level with the ranch, a dog barked a couple of times, but not urgently and then stopped. Harker smiled, for he'd had a dog once which also chased rabbits in its dreams.

When he reached the road, he unhitched his horse, remounted and sat for a while picturing in his mind what would be happening back at the lake. Water would be cascading down the mountain and collecting in the basin which would hold it fine. But it wouldn't hold it forever. The amount coming in was now much greater than the amount flowing out. As the level rose, so would the pressure on the dam which would groan, shift and eventually give way. Tons of water suddenly released would destroy anything in its path.

Viall's ranch-house and outbuildings were in its path.

He waited a while longer. The night sky was now pale and the stars were fading. Suddenly making up his mind, he took his Colt from its holster, raised it and fired three shots in the air. Three shots should wake 'em up. He didn't intend to kill anybody, just send a shot over Viall's bows, slow him down a mite. Then he rode off fast the way he'd come, heading back to Laureston.

★ ★ ★

It was just beginning to get light when old Jedediah Parsons, who always had to be up before anyone else, climbed into his pants and boots, lit the stove in the cook-shack and went out to collect wood for the stove to make the coffee that started the day.

When he got outside, he sensed there was something different about the place. At first he couldn't make out what it was. Then he was aware that the stream was making a noise, a bigger noise than usual. He took a peek. It was foaming and running fuller and faster than usual too. It was racing. He climbed up to the dam and what he saw scared him almost to death.

The dam was overflowing.

Water spurted out of the base and at various points of the rock-and-lumber wall. It splashed over the top, spilled over the corners and what was flowing out of the base was no longer a gentle stream but a roaring torrent. Pressure was building up inside the basin. The dam had never been made to hold back such a weight of water. The timbers groaned, the rocks would have to give. They wouldn't last much longer, and when the dam burst . . .

Jedediah turned and ran down towards the ranch house hollering his head off. He still had fifty yards to go when he heard three shots.

Harker's three shots jerked Walter Viall into wakefulness. Then he too heard the roar and other voices shouting warnings. Mikey Viall burst through the door and screamed at his pa to get up and get out. Viall did not stop to ask questions.

Outside, men were running every

which way. He shouted for them to open the stable doors, get away from the buildings and make for higher ground. They made a hundred yards to safety, stopped and turned to look.

They were in time to see a wall of water swell out of nowhere and smash into the wooden buildings. When it had gone, roofs had been stove in, walls hung at drunken angles and one barn had been carried away altogether. Timber was spread out everywhere, like matchsticks. No one said anything.

Viall came out of the shock first.

'This was no accident!' he snarled. 'Mikey, send someone up to check the outflow sluices. I'll bet a dollar to a cent they're wide open!'

Rube, his face still red and puffy from his encounter with Harker, rushed up.

'Pa,' he said, 'there was a lot of stuff stored in the barns. In the house too. Doesn't look like we'll salvage much. You want me to check?'

Viall nodded, but his mind was elsewhere.

Who would pull a stunt like this? In all the time he'd been moving up through the ranks in Laureston, no one had ever tried anything on him. They were all too scared. They didn't have the guts for it. So what was new that had changed things? He didn't have far to look.

'Harker!' he mouthed grimly.

The man had killed Zeke and bested him twice. He remembered a saying: never two without three. Viall aimed to prove it wrong. Harker had got the better of him first in a private room of Tabitha Strafford's hotel and now on his very own doorstep. He swore there'd be no third time.

'Get dressed and saddle up!' he yelled. 'We're going to town.'

Rube came back, shaking his head, saying most of the stuff was lost but the animals hadn't come to much harm.

'Leave that to the boys to sort out. I got a job for you. When the news that I've been made to look like a drowned rat gets out, the whole town will laugh.

I can't have that. So I'm going to tighten the screws on the town and everybody in Tate County, so they know no one fools around with Walter Viall. I want you to go over to Jake Stone's place. He's behind with his rent. Remind him. And don't you go gentle.'

Then to Mikey he barked, 'Go get Pat Murtagh!'

★ ★ ★

As he rode, Harker thought about what he was going to say to Tabitha. She said she had an understanding with Walter Viall. The first thing would be to find out what that 'understanding' was, exactly. It couldn't be the obvious thing most folk would think of. First, he didn't figure her for that kind of woman and second, from what he'd heard and seen of the man, Viall wasn't that sort of man. Anyway, if Walt was seriously interested in chasing skirts, he had the money to buy himself all the soiled doves he wanted: there were always plenty waiting around and available, less sassy girls who wouldn't answer back and make life hard for him.

But Harker was also curious to know how a sister of Billy Boden had ended up in Laureston running a hotel. That sort of business took financing. Where'd she got the money to set it up? Who had staked her?

He dropped his horse off at Bishop's livery stable to be fed and watered, then walked down the street to the hotel. It was quiet but already open for business. But it was too early for any other than a few hardened drinkers. Tabitha was up and about.

'We need to talk,' said Harker.

She looked at him hard.

'I thought I told you to leave town,' she said.

'I'm the sort of man who doesn't take kindly to doing what he's told.'

'And what did the army have to say about that?'

'I had complaints,' said Harker with a grin. 'The sergeant said he didn't like my manner. It's early. How about some coffee while we talk?'

Calling over to her barkeep to bring a pot of coffee, she turned and led him to one of the back rooms that served as her office. She sat behind a desk and stared at him again.

'Situation's changed,' said Harker.

'What situation?'

'You said you've been holding Viall back. Claimed you had an understanding with him. After what happened yesterday, I figure whatever your 'understanding' was is now a busted flush. Viall went after Billy. He wanted an answer out of him. I guess the question was whether he was going to sell up or not. You know as well as I do that Billy will never give in to bully-boy tactics. So you must know Viall would have killed him if I hadn't happened along.'

Her face clouded.

'You're right. Walt and I have an agreement — '

'You don't have agreements with a

man like Viall. He never keeps his side of any bargain.'

'I know that. But I really thought I had him nailed.'

'Well, he just un-nailed himself. What is this agreement, anyway? You can tell me. Whatever it is, or was, Viall just tore it up.'

She hesitated.

'If you like,' said Harker, 'you can start by telling me how you came to be proprietor of a hotel in Laureston. Ain't many women in that line of work.'

'I don't see that it's any of your damn business,' she answered coolly, 'but I'll tell you. It's no secret. It was left to me.'

'You inherited it? From an uncle?'

'From my husband. He won it in a poker game.'

'You're husband's dead?' said Harker. 'How'd he die?'

'He was gunned down a week after the game. It happened right here, in Laureston. Didn't Abe Monkman tell you the tale the other night? It was one of his biggest stories.'

'I'd like to hear it from you, if it's not too painful to tell.'

'There's not much to tell. Girl meets boy back east, girl marries boy, girl and boy decide to make a new life out west. They join a wagon train. The wagon train gets robbed by raiders. Girl and boy lose all their goods and are stranded here, in Laureston. This was before Billy and Martha came out. One night Andy took my wedding ring and the last of the cash we'd put by and sat in on a game in the bar. Our plan was: win and move on, lose and we'd stay. But that night Andy just couldn't lose. He won a couple of thousand dollars, cleaned out the opposition. Only Abner Morgan was left in. He owned the place in those days. He should have known better but just as some men can't stop drinking Abner was a gambling man. Anyway, Andy walked away from the table the new owner of Laureston's only hotel.'

'And a week later?'

'It was around eleven in the morning.

Andy stepped out to take a look at a horse he was buying from Ed Bishop down at the stables. A rider came through, pulled a gun, shot him in the back, then rode off.'

'Sheriff do anything about it?'

'It all happened so fast. No one saw anything. But I did. I was standing in the door, just about to ask him something. I couldn't find the cellar key and thought he had it. The man who shot Andy was small and wore a green shirt. That's all I can remember.'

Tom Harker said, 'That's a sorry tale, ma'am — '

'And that's all of it. No, not all . . . '

She offered to refill Harker's cup. He nodded and said 'Please!'

'I told you how the wagon train we were with was held up. Know who the robbers were? Mundy's Marauders.'

Harker gave a start. Mundy had been a Confederate Colonel on the losing side of the war. When the shooting stopped, he refused to accept defeat and went on fighting. He fought everyone, the victors because they had won and his own side because they had lost. He got together a gang of very tough ex-soldiers and wreaked mayhem over three states burning, murdering, stealing, kidnapping, robbing trains and rustling cattle and sheep. He ran what was a small army. There was a price on his head. Then a United States marshal got on his trail and tracked him down to a spread in Utah. There was a shoot-out and Mundy got killed. A lot of his men died but some got away. Every last man of them was wanted. Bounty hunters had gone after them and gunned down a few. But three or four were still unaccounted for.

'And one of them is Walter Viall,' said Tabitha.

Harker almost choked on his coffee.

'Does he know you know?' asked Harker.

'Yes. I told him.'

'How come you're still breathing?'

'Let me tell it my way. When we fetched up here at Laureston, Walt was pretty well dug in and getting big ideas. He'd started pushing out the settlers who'd bought up government land for $1.25 an acre and was building up the spread he had on the Santa Fe road.

'Then one day, he came into the saloon with some of his men. Walked straight up to Andy and started threatening him. He said that Laureston was his town, that he aimed to be a power in the land, that he wanted the hotel. He didn't say he'd like to buy it. He said he was going to 'acquire' it and Andy could get out if he didn't like it. Andy said he was staying. He was shot the next day.'

'And you think Viall was behind it?' asked Harker.

'Of course. Andy knew Walt wouldn't take no for an answer. He said we should make a written statement testifying to the fact that Walter Viall had a price on his head. We'd give time, place and names of some of the other folks who were attacked with us when our wagons were burned out. Then we'd send it to a lawyer for safekeeping with instructions to open it if anything happened to us. Andy got killed before he could do it. But after the funeral, I did exactly like he said. Abe Monkman gave me the name of a lawyer in Acre Creek. Then I went to Walt and faced him down. I said I knew who he was, that if anything happened to me, the law would be on his trail five minutes later. He believed me. I could see he wanted me out of the way but it was too risky. He couldn't just take off and start up somewhere else where no one knew him. He'd invested too much time and money here. Then a few months later Billy and Martha came out on a visit, liked the place and stayed.'

'And every time he got too close to you and yours,' said Harker, 'whenever he started to lean too hard on Billy, you reminded him that all you had to do was say the word and he was dead meat? Lady, you play dangerous games.'

'Why? It's worked up to now. I'm still here.'

'But it looks like the magic's worn off. He's stopped being scared. Now why would that be?'

'Could be he just lost his temper, went for Billy because he got tired of holding back — '

'Men like Viall don't go off at half-cock. They have a long fuse where their interests are concerned. No, ma'am, it looks to me like something's happened.'

He thought a moment: 'Try this: Abe told me Viall's got political ambitions. Maybe he's made powerful friends at county level or even in the State legislature. Maybe he's used his money and contacts to scare off lawyers who make a nuisance of themselves or bought himself a sheriff or two, or judges who'll make sure courts look the other way. Could be Walt figures the law can't touch him. It's been known to happen.'

'If it has,' said Tabitha, 'we're in trouble.'

'So is Billy. Viall has tried to

strong-arm him once. No reason to think he won't try again. At the moment, Billy's on his own up at Bluewater with Martha, the baby and the Doc. I'm going out there right now. And I think you should come with me. It ain't safe for you to stay in town any more.'

'Don't worry about me, I'll be fine. If Walt comes here looking for trouble, I can handle him.'

Harker thought of reasoning with her but didn't. Tabitha had a mind of her own and grit to spare. She was plain ornery — though that was the only plain thing about her.

6

The Green Shirt

Harker retrieved his horse from Ed Bishop's stables, swung up into the saddle and took the road to Bluewater Valley.

An hour after he'd gone, Walt Viall and a dozen of his men galloped into town, yelling, firing shots in the air, frightening horses and townspeople alike.

They walked right into Jepson's bank, lawyer Benson's office, the bureau of Abe Monkman's *Gazette*, grabbing papers off desks, throwing them around, breaking windows and smashing chairs. In Sam Whipple's store, they wiped goods off the shelves onto the floor, shot up bags of flour and beans, smashed jars of preserves and pickle and emptied boxes of nails and coffee onto the counter. They sat down in Ma Kelly's eating-house and ordered breakfast. They ate what they wanted and threw the rest, still on the plates, at the wall. Viall watched them at work from the boardwalk outside the hotel where Sheriff Rukatch found him.

'Call 'em off, Viall,' he growled. 'What's going on?'

'The boys are all riled up, Sheriff,' said Viall. 'And come to think of it, so am I.'

'So riled with Laureston they want to take the town apart?'

'Before you start lecturing me about being a good citizen, tell me where you were at around dawn? No don't bother, because I know where you weren't. You weren't anywhere near when my spread got demolished by a wall of water that wasn't no accident! If the law isn't there when it's needed, to stop bad men doing real bad things, what's to stop an aggrieved party spreading a little of the misery around!'

Rukatch caught sight of a plume of

103

smoke further down the street.

'I said call 'em off,' he said, waving his gun at Viall, 'or I'll make a few holes in your hide and let out some of that hot air that's got into you.'

Viall looked at him and reached for his gun. For a moment it was as if he was going to kick up rough. Then he relaxed and fired three shots in the air which hit only a passing cloud. At his signal, the ruckus started to die down.

'I'll buy you a drink, Sheriff,' he said, 'and put you in the picture.'

* * *

Jake Stone was forty, bald, hard-working. His wife was thirty-five, with hair that was no longer young, like the rest of her, and a figure that was not so much slender as lean from grinding hard work. Clinging to her skirts were Jenny and young Bobby, who was holding a doe-eyed spaniel on a lead made from a length of frayed old rope: Patch, his pet and the love of his young life. The whole family had come out on to the porch of their cabin when the riders arrived.

'The old man told me to call round,' said Rube, without dismounting.

'If it's business,' said Jake, 'you'd best come inside.'

'That's right,' said Mrs Stone pleasantly. 'You can talk better out of the sun. I'll fix some coffee.'

'No coffee,' said Rube curtly. 'I don't need no coffee to tell you what I got to say. Pa says you're behind with the rent. What you got to say to that?'

'I ain't behind with no rent,' said Jake, breaking into a sweat. 'Paid up last first of the month like I always do. Nobody more regular than me.'

'You calling my Pa a liar?' said Rube, leaning forward in his saddle as if trying to fill his nose with the smell of the man's fear.

'I sure ain't,' said Jake. 'Just saying there's some mistake. All the truth I know is that I paid up on time. There's no rent owed.'

'Pa says there is. Now if you was me, who would you believe? Walter Viall, biggest cattleman in Tate County, or some two-bit campesino living on a flea-bitten strip of land that ain't his own any more, with a dog-faced wife and a couple of runts?'

Jake paled. He had a choice. He wasn't wearing a gun, but he could take on Rube Viall and five of his pa's armed men single-handed with one hand and shelter his wife and kids with the other. Or he could swallow what Rube had just said.

He swallowed, though it almost choked him.

'I've paid Walt Viall all I owe till next time. Even if I was minded to pay twice, I couldn't. Cupboard's all bare.'

'So you won't pay,' snarled Rube.

Jake's boy started to cry, scared by the big man's voice and the hard expression in his face.

'Shut the kid up,' Rube yelled.

His anger communicated itself to his dog which ran forward to the end of its rope, barking. The barking made Rube's horse snort, shy and almost unseat its rider. Bobby called for Patch to quit all that noise, then yanked on the rope, to pull him back, but the rope broke and quick as a knife the dog was between the horse's legs, yapping and nipping, causing no damage but doing a powerful amount of scaring.

'Here, Patch!' the boy called, 'you just stop that!'

Jake Stone started forward, reached for the dog that was maddening the horse and pulled him out, getting kicked on the left forearm for his pains. He gave the end of the rope to Bobby and told him to make sure and keep a good hold on it then held out his right hand to Rube who, in the confusion, had landed on his backside in the dust.

But Rube fended him off, got to his feet and brushed himself down.

'Sure am sorry, Rube,' said Stone. 'The dog got scared and the rope broke.'

'Come inside,' said Mrs Stone. 'I'll

get water and you can get cleaned up.'

Bobby had picked up the dog and was holding it in his arms. It was still showing its teeth and yapping and struggling to get free.

Rube went on brushing himself. His face was flushed with anger. He'd been made to look a fool in front of his men who, as he could see out of the corner of his eye, were having difficulty keeping straight faces. He'd been made to feel small by the puppy dog belonging to a runt sired by a rent-dodging nobody who could have hidden all his worldly possessions under a duck.

Then the dog burst out of Bobby's clutches and went back to worrying Rube's horse which panicked, reared up, turned and galloped off.

Rube took out his gun and shot the dog.

Bobby screamed and ran to where Patch lay bleeding on to the dust. He picked him up. The dog's head swung and its legs flopped as the boy walked back to the house with him. There were tears in his eyes.

'You shot my dog. You're just a big bully, mister,' he said to Rube.

'He's right,' said Mrs Stone. 'Bobby loved that dog and you just killed him because you could. You're not welcome here. You'd better go.'

'Who's going to make me,' said Rube, like some kid in a playground stand-off. 'Anyway, I ain't going before I either get Pa's rent or some equivalent satisfaction.'

'You done enough for one day,' said Jake, disgust overcoming caution. 'Just go.'

'I'll go, if that's the way you want it.'

One of his men had chased Rube's horse and brought it back. He hauled himself up into the saddle and dug its ribs with both heels. His men followed. All four Stones watched them go, then turned and went back inside the house.

Rube called a halt as soon as he was out of sight of the Stones' cabin. He ordered his men to round up as many beeves as they could find. The range was not big but the grazing was good. Within an hour, Rube and his boys had gathered up maybe four hundred head, mostly White Face, which Jake Stone was tending for Walt Viall. The herd was worth a lot of money and it was part of Viall's stock of White Face, which he favoured over the longhorn because the breed carried more meat.

When Rube figured they had got together enough animals for the purpose, he gave the word. His five hands got behind the herd and started whooping and hollering and whistling. The steers jumped, rolled their eyes and started running. Whips and gunshots kept the leaders on track, and where the front steers went, the rest followed. And the route they were following, led them directly to the fences, barns and cabin which Jake Stone had built up from nothing.

Jake heard the rumble. He could not figure out what it was until he looked out the window and saw the stampede coming his way. He reached for his rifle, ran across the patch of dirt that fronted his house and got to the fence before he fired. He shot the leading steer which fell and brought four or five others with it. The herd hesitated a moment and started to turn. But outriders emerged through the churned-up dust and they goaded the herd back on course. Jake could not understand why riders would deliberately want to guide runaway steers towards fences and buildings where there were people. It made no sense. Then suddenly it did.

Rube was aiming the stampede at his home, using the herd like a weapon. Jake shot the new leader, but the riders again reset the charging steers. He got off a couple more shots, aiming this time at the riders. He winged one, he thought, then turned to run. But he was only halfways back to the house when the frontrunners were on him. The rest flowed over him, divided when they reached the cabin, where Mrs Stone and her children crouched in terror, and then were gone, leaving only a cloud of dust and a fading thunder of hoofs as they galloped away into the distance.

As the dust settled, Mrs Stone saw that the fence had disappeared and the barns had been flattened. Not fifteen yards from their front door lay the still, bloody, broken body of her husband.

★ ★ ★ .

'So you reckon them sluices was raised deliberate?' said Rukatch, pouring another drink.

'Like I said, it warn't no accident.'

'Got anyone in mind as perpetrator of the deed?' asked Rukatch, who hid the smile he was feeling under the frown he wore on his official face. Harker! It couldn't be anybody else!

'I have my suspicions, but I'm not a man to make wild accusations. I'll bide my time until I've got evidence.'

The day Viall showed respect for any part of the law process, thought

Rukatch, the whole of mankind would have entered on to higher plane of decency.

'Besides, I got something else to do today. I got to bury Zeke, my boy. Gutman fixed to be at the cemetery with him and the minister for three o'clock.'

'All the more reason for keeping your boys quiet. It would show proper respect.'

Judge Morton had signed the order for releasing the body first thing. He was still studying the details. The case was complex. Had Harker killed in self-defence? Was Zeke the unidentified sniper who'd accounted for five other travellers? But whether there was enough evidence or not to make a case, there was a body and bodies had to be buried. Bodies don't keep.

So just before three in the afternoon, Viall, his two sons and most of the men on his payroll trooped into Laureston cemetery to pay their last respects. They all removed their hats. But no one looked very cut up about it, not even Viall who'd always put Zeke down as the most stupid of his boys, none of whom had any brains. Viall blamed the late Mrs Viall for that.

The minister had just said that man is born to die and that all is vanity, and close relatives had tossed a handful of dirt into the grave, when there was a disturbance at the cemetery gates. Viall looked up angrily to identify the source and saw Mrs Stone.

'Murderer!' she yelled. 'Coward!'

Motioning the minister to cut the proceedings short, Viall crammed his brown derby back on his head and strode to where Mrs Stone, accompanied by Abe Monkman, was waiting for him. As he approached she stopped yelling and made an effort to compose herself for the confrontation.

'You got something to say to me, Mrs Stone? If you just stay calm a spell, I'll answer whatever you got to say to me. But yelling and carrying on don't help none.'

But since Mrs Stone was now perfectly composed, Viall's words fell flat.

'My husband is dead, Mr Viall,' she said with dignity, 'and my children have no father. If it is so, and I tell you it is, it is of your doing.'

'I'm mighty sorry to hear of your loss, ma'am, but I can't be held accountable. I been here in Laureston all day. I came to bury my boy Zeke who was murdered day before yesterday. If Jake's dead like you say, then I guess you will understand my feelings too at this sad time. So perhaps you'll excuse me while I go mourn my boy.'

He made as if to walk round her, but she stepped sideways into his path.

'You hypocrite!' she said coldly. 'You know no more about feelings than a dead rattlesnake! Sure, you didn't kill Jake with your bare hands, you ain't got the guts for it, but you ordered it done. Where is he? Where's that ugly, pudding-faced excuse for a man that calls himself your son? Where's Ruben?'

'Here,' said Rube from behind his father's shoulder. 'Why're you asking? And be more polite. I don't care to be called names.'

'Just hold it there, folks,' said Sheriff Rukatch. 'It ain't seemly to be staging a slanging match here in the graveyard. I want all of you in my office, where we can see if we can get to the bottom of this.'

Hanging on Abe's arm, Mrs Stone turned and followed the sheriff. Viall, Rube and two or three of his men brought up the rear. The rest shrugged then made for the hotel where Walter Viall had promised a wake.

When they were in his office, Rukatch said: 'Sit yourself down, ma'am, and tell me what happened.'

Mrs Stone, sometimes with tears running down her cheek, at others with a tremble about her chin and a quiver in her voice, told the sheriff how Rube had been sent by his father and had demanded, with menaces, payment of rent that had already been paid, how he'd lost his temper with Bobby's spaniel, how he'd deliberately stampeded the herd at their house, which was how Jake had been trampled to death.

Rube said Mrs Stone was making it all up and denied everything. Viall said the Stones didn't owe him a penny, seeing that the rent was fully paid up to date, so there was no reason for him to put the strong arm on Jake. He added that he would vouch for Rube a hundred per cent. He was a good son and a real smart boy.

'Of course,' he added, 'if there's third-party witnesses to say different, then that would put another colour on it. But if there's nobody to confirm what Mrs Stone says happened, then we'll never get any further. It's just her word against mine.'

'Mrs Stone,' asked Rukatch, 'was there anybody else there, not connected with Mr Viall, who could back you up?'

Mrs Stone bit her lip, shook 'no' with her head, and looked away, defeated.

'I'll put the facts such as they are to Judge Morton,' said Rukatch, 'and see what he's got to say. That agreeable to both parties?'

'Absolutely,' said Viall. 'We can't just let this lie. First, there's the whole question of the compensation that's owed me.'

The sheriff raised an eyebrow, Mrs Stone reacted as if she'd been struck by a thunderbolt and Abe's eyebrows came together in the deepest frown he ever frowned.

'No need to look so surprised,' said Viall. 'If Rube didn't stampede the herd that destroyed fences and buildings that rightly belong to me, then what did? A man could just as easy speculate that Jake did something to spook the herd and brought it all on himself. I don't mean he did it on purpose. He could have tripped and his gun could have gone off by accident. I'd need to cost the damage to my property and establish how many head I've lost in this business.'

'Good God!' said Abe. 'What sort of man are you? Jake Stone is dead, your own son has only just been laid to rest, and all you can think of is money!'

'Not all, Abe,' said Viall with a smile. 'There's another matter at stake here: my reputation.'

'You got no reputation,' said Abe, 'except that of a ruthless man of business.'

'You shouldn't go round making remarks like that, Abe, you being a newspaperman and supposed to be impartial. But I'll let that pass. You're all het up. But I'm serious. Solid citizens here in Laureston, and also as far away as Acre Creek, have made an approach asking me to put up as a candidate for the office of county recorder this fall, in the November election. I ain't made my mind if I'll run yet. But in the circumstances I can't afford to have allegations, however unsubstantiated, hanging over me just now. I hope you'll bear that in mind, Abe, when the *Gazette* gets round to reporting whether I'm going to stand or not. You'll be the first to know, incidentally.'

There was a silence. Sheriff Rukatch broke it:

'Don't look like we're going anyplace with this. So I want both parties to step across to Judge Morton and make their statements so he can decide if there's a charge to answer. Then we'll ride on up to Mrs Stone's place for a look-see.'

Mrs Stone looked suddenly deflated, weighed down by the thought that her word was not enough, that justice was not for the poor, that she, who had lost everything, might yet be called on to pay compensation to a man who did not want for money. Viall was rich, of the race who are always so well protected by the laws of the land. Such men can afford lawyers and lawyers can twist a right into a wrong and a wrong into a right without raising a sweat. For his part, Walter Viall knew he had all the aces in his hand. The more thought he gave it, the more he liked the thought.

By this time, a small crowd of townspeople, attracted by the hubbub, had gathered outside the sheriff's office. They had just been joined by the owner of Laureston's only hotel.

'What's this all about?' Tabitha asked Abe as he started down the street with the others.

He told her and what he said rocked her back on her heels. She'd known Walter Viall a long time. He'd always been a bully and he'd never shown any respect for the law. He'd lied in court, he'd fixed public auctions, he'd most likely put his WV brand on heifers that belonged to other men. She suspected but couldn't prove that he'd had a hand in her husband's murder. But since then, she'd never known him to use violence. He'd kept his nose clean.

But maybe Harker was right. Maybe something had happened that made Viall feel safe, gave him the feeling that he was out of reach of the law. If he was thinking of going into politics, maybe he'd done important men a favour here and a service there which he could call in whenever he needed to get out of a fix.

'Listen, Abe,' she said. 'I don't like any of this. It seems like Walt's taken the gloves off. He always was mean. He just got a lot meaner and I want to know why. He's using murder as a way of doing business.'

Then out of the corner of her eye she saw a rider dismount and hitch his horse to the rail outside the hotel. He said something to Mikey Viall who'd ridden in with him. They both laughed. They glanced casually across at the knot of people outside the sheriffs office which was now dispersing.

She didn't know the man, but there was something familiar about him. He was small. Then she knew him.

'Who's the man with Mikey across the street. Short, wearing the green shirt.'

Abe looked up.

'Him? That's Pat Murtagh. You don't

want to go messing with him. He's a professional gun with a reputation as a cold-blooded killer. Now what's he doing here so pally with one of the Viall boys?'

7

Manhunt

Billy Boden was tough. He could go without sleep. He had reserves of stamina. But he'd taken a lot of punishment which, when added to older injuries he hadn't got over, left him feeling pretty weak. But Doc Prentice reckoned he'd live. The Doc had ridden back to Laureston. The way things were shaping up, he said, he'd soon be getting a lot of customers and couldn't afford to be out of town when he was most needed.

Martha busied around, feeding her husband up, seeing he kept rested. Already, there was colour in his face and his muscles were acquiring a definite tone.

'Just listen to that gal!' he grinned at Harker. 'Bossing me around! I've known regimental sergeants who went easier on men!'

Harker's tale of how he'd drowned the Viall ranch lit a flame of optimism which had not been seen on the Bluewater Valley range in a long spell. So it was from a house of good cheer that he rode out early next morning, bound for Laureston, where he was aiming to hook up with Rukatch. Maybe they could fire up the men the sheriff had mentioned, the ones who didn't like Viall's way of operating. Even if they couldn't muster enough to give him a regular stand-up fight, then maybe they could start a campaign of guerrilla attacks that would slow him down, cost him money, get under his skin. Wasn't the lion that could lick every beast in the jungle driven mad by fleas?

He was thinking about tactics when somebody shot at him. He looked up and saw four riders heading his way at a gallop not a hundred yards off. They'd been waiting behind a rock. Now they were in the open. Their intentions weren't friendly.

Harker took in at a glance Rube Viall and two men in check shirts, the kind Sam Whipple and every other shopkeeper in the county sold in their stores. Viall's men, no doubt about it. The fourth man, who was either short or rode low over his horse, had on a green shirt. Four men chasing. Harker didn't stay to watch any more but heeled his horse and headed for higher ground.

As he turned, he heard more shots. One spanged off a rock to his left, but mostly the shooting was wild and in any case the firing stopped when they dropped behind and were hidden in a dip. Then he was out of sight in dense timber where he was forced to slow down. He struck an animal trail. He was tempted to turn and follow it. Instead, he crossed it, held his course for a hundred yards, turned left down sloping ground for another fifty, then doubled right back up until he struck the animal trail again further along. This time, he stayed on it and soon was gaining height.

Harker knew a yard or two about covering his tracks and throwing chasers off the scent. If it was a manhunt they wanted, he grinned, he'd give them one.

The timber stopped at a level stretch of ground littered with rocky outcrops. There was now no sign of pursuit. But Harker knew better than to think that the riders, still battling for his trail with the dense woodland, had given up on him. He rode in small circles, criss-crossing this way and that, trampling his hoof-marks in the turf. Then he spurred his horse up a steep slope, reined in a few yards over the other side of the crest and dismounted once he reckoned he was out of sight. He dropped on to his stomach, crawled forward and looked down.

He watched for maybe twenty minutes before seeing four men emerge from the timber. They saw his tracks but were clearly confused. With a shout, Rube set off on a false trail but stopped when he found it led back to the circles.

The two check shirts rode round and round staring at the ground. The man in the green shirt just sat on his horse, waiting. Once he looked up at the hill which Harker had chosen as a vantage point but gave no sign that he had noticed anything.

Harker sighed. If he was going to teach these varmints a thing or two, he was going to have to give them a helping hand. For he knew now what he was going to do: teach those boys a lesson they wouldn't forget in a hurry. He got to his feet and showed himself.

Immediately, the green shirt's head went up and the other three looked at where he pointed. Then he dug his spurs into his horse's ribs and his companions did likewise. But by the time they reached the top of the slope, Harker was out of sight. They followed his trail, which led down to a stream. So far so good. Hoof prints showed up clearly where he had entered the water, but there were none on the opposite bank to show where he had come out.

Rube and the green shirt rode upstream and the two check shirts rode down the other way. By the time they found the place where their quarry had got back on to dry land, they'd lost any chance of getting a sight of him. Moreover, Harker had chosen the spot on purpose. Under water in the rainy season, the riverside was now just a beach of dry stones which didn't take a trail.

The four men combed the beach for stones which had been disturbed or turned over. Eventually, they made a connection and rode on, following a trail that even a one-eyed man could not have missed in the dark.

They set off at a fast lick but after a while slowed their pace, for their prey was covering lots of miles and their horses were tiring.

The land began to change. The good level grazing strewn with rocky scars turned into gently undulating folds with small streams in the bottoms and groves of willow at intervals along their banks. Then the ground began to rise and turned into the foothills of the Blue Mountains. Here the timber reappeared. The pines grew thick all the way up to the foot of high sandstone bluffs which sprang out of them like huge pillars on which giant gates might once have been hung. And all the while, the marks of Harker's passage through the landscape stood out as clear as the veins in a drunk's nose.

In the end, even so visible a trail became impossible to follow in the fading light. It led straight into timber where the rising moon would not penetrate. The manhunters called a halt at the edge of the forest.

Harker had waited for them, knowing that they'd have to bed down there for the night. He had already picked out a likely place for his own camp among the trees on a level patch of ground in a hollow next to a bush-shrouded brook maybe 300 yards downwind from the edge of the woods. He tethered his horse so that it wouldn't stray and, leaving it to feed, crept back the way he'd come. He watched his pursuers make their way wearily towards him. When they reached the woods, they paused. Through the darkening branches, Harker got a clear view of the four men and heard them arguing. Rube was all fired up and wanted to go on. The man in the green shirt was small and compactly built. He let Rube sound off and then, without a word, removed his horse's saddle. They would camp here for the night. The other two did not disagree with the man they called Pat. Pat took out the makings and smoked while the others hobbled the horses and set up camp.

Satisfied they weren't going anywhere, Harker went back to his camp which was in a hollow and downwind. No danger in lighting a fire. He hadn't eaten since breakfast and the mountain air had put an edge on his appetite. He had no supplies or bedroll with him. He'd been on his way to see Rukatch, dammit, and a man doesn't take a week's supplies and a pack when going into town to pay a social call. But Harker knew how to live off the land. He set about supper using an old Indian trick.

He plucked three or four hairs from his tethered pony's tail and with his knife nicked out a small piece of leather from his waistcoat. He tied the leather on to the end of the hairs instead of a worm and a hook. Then he dangled his line in the water and waited. Soon dozens of small fish appeared, drawn by curiosity to inspect the dancing bait. When one bit, its teeth got caught in the leather and could not free itself. Once it was firmly hooked, Harker gently lifted it out. When he'd caught enough, he cut willow twigs, speared the fish and stuck the twigs upright around the fire, turning them until they were done. They tasted good, though instead of water he would have given a lot for a pot of hot, strong coffee to wash them down with.

While his fish were cooking, he returned briefly to see what his pursuers were doing. They had a fire lit and were sitting around it, smoking. In its glow, he could just make out their unsaddled, hobbled horses grazing on leaves and grass. Harker smiled: those nags were getting more of a supper than their riders who hadn't eaten any more than they had all day. There was plenty of game about, but they wouldn't shoot a jackrabbit for fear the noise would give their position away.

'What's he playing at?' said one of the check shirts. 'He's leading us a merry dance and that's the truth.'

'Now whyever would he do that, Newman?' said Rube. 'Way I see it, he's running scared. He don't know what he's doing. There ain't no sense to his movements. He goes this way, then that way, riding over his own tracks. If he was doing it on purpose, he'd have lost us a long time ago. No, he's just a rabbit running scared.'

Harker smiled, but he noted that the man in the green shirt kept his own counsel.

'I say we let him go,' said the other check shirt. 'Tomorrow we hightail it out of here, right? Ain't no reason why tomorrow won't be different from today. Harker may be running scared, like Rube says, or he could be playing games. Either way we got no supplies and we cain't hunt him down on an empty belly.'

At this point, the fourth man spoke. His voice was light and sat well on his Irish brogue.

'And there was me thinking all you Americans was all tough hombres that never gave up on what they started. Walt gave us a job to do. I say we don't turn round until we've done it. So shut you're squawking gobs and get some sleep. Hayes, you take first watch. Wake Rube to replace you in two hours, then it'll be Newman and then me. We don't want any surprises.'

The words were said pleasantly enough. But there was no mistaking the menace in them. The men caught it and, cowed, prepared to turn in. Rube threw more wood on the fire. It blazed up.

Harker returned to his camp, ate his supper and slept for an hour.

Then he crept quietly back to the camp at the edge of the woods.

★ ★ ★

The spring morning came cold and bright.

Pat Murtagh opened one eye. The fire was dead and Hayes was snoring at his post. No one was on guard. Rube and Newman were still asleep with their heads on their saddles. They hadn't moved from where they were when they'd settled down for the night.

Warily, he reached for his gun. His hands were stiff with cold. His keen senses detected nothing that spelled danger. He relaxed, got to his feet walked over to Hayes and kicked him savagely in the ribs.

Hayes came awake with a howl of pain. Rube and Newman jerked into consciousness and sat up blinking.

'We got through the night without being killed, but it's no thanks to you, Hayes.'

'Sorry, Pat,' he said. 'Must have dropped off.'

'In the army, you'd have been shot for that. Get the fire going again. Then go shoot us a jackrabbit or whatever edible is up and about at this time.'

'What about Harker?' said Rube. 'When he hears the shot, he'll know it's us, for sure. Ain't nobody else about up this high in the mountains.'

'It ain't night no more, Rube, or didn't you notice? He won't come creeping up on us now it's light.'

Hayes threw dead branches on to the embers, fanned them with his hat and soon a red flame licked upward. Then he got up and went to shoot breakfast. He was back inside a minute. He was holding several lengths of cut rope.

'Pat!' he said, panting. 'The horses are gone! The hobbles were cut!'

'Harker!' said Murtagh, and he

swore. 'He was here! He could have shot us while we slept. But he took the horses instead.'

His face was grim. He'd never doubted for a moment that Harker was stringing them along. But here was proof. He'd been made a fool of. Suddenly rage boiled over.

He grabbed one of the rope lengths from Hayes and laid it hard across his face, splitting his cheek open and only just missing his left eye.

'I said go and shoot a jackrabbit. When I give an order, I want it obeyed. Next time, I'll kill you!'

The other two men watched as the blood started to flow, stunned by the suddenness and viciousness of the attack, which scared them.

'And you, Newman, scout around and see if you can pick up a trail. Shouldn't be hard: single rider leading four horses should leave a trail as wide as the Missouri River.'

Murtagh's face was grim.

Newman opened his mouth, then

thought better of it and went.

'Rube, you go take a look around too.'

Rube did as he was told.

Newman wasn't gone long.

'Which way did he go?' asked Murtagh.

'Looks like the horses were led off deeper into the trees. You want me to go after him?'

They heard a pistol crack as a jackrabbit died. Hayes, his kerchief wrapped around his cheek to stem the bleeding, returned, skinned and spitted his kill and propped it over the fire on two forked sticks. He sat on his heels watching it. Blood fell in drips from the kerchief.

Rube came back. He'd stumbled across the same trail Newman had seen. He'd followed it to the hollow where Harker had camped. The ashes of the fire were still warm, he said, but there was no sign of Harker or their horses. But there was a trail that led out of the camp and it headed back to the open prairie they'd ridden across the day before.

The jackrabbit was ready. Hayes put out his hand to take the spit off the fire.

There was a blur around Murtagh's holster, then his gun was in his hand and firing. A bullet raised dust just by Hayes's right foot.

'No breakfast for you,' snarled Murtagh, putting up his smoking gun. 'You don't deserve breakfast, you never earned no damn breakfast!'

Rube and Newman stared open-mouthed at him. They'd never seen such speed and controlled aggression.

So Hayes got no breakfast. Anyway, he'd suddenly lost his appetite. He jumped when Pat spoke again:

'I got a job for you,' he said, pointing to a tall pine at the edge of the forest. 'Get up that there tree and tell us what you see. I want to know if he's headed back the way we came.'

Hayes moved off while his three companions ate up the jackrabbit which, though a fully grown buck, didn't fill a belly.

The pine was tall, an easy climb, with plenty of hand-and foot-holds. Hayes moved up the trunk quickly.

As he disappeared from sight, Murtagh tossed the last of the jackrabbit bones into the fire and stood up. Then he began gathering up broken branches and tree debris which he piled round the base of the pine. He barked an order and Rube and Newman started to do the same.

'Ain't no need for this, Pat,' said Newman. 'Hayes is nimble as a bag of monkeys. He don't need all this to break a fall, cos he ain't going to fall.'

Murtagh didn't reply but took a brand from the fire and pushed it into the brushwood heaped around the trunk. It caught at once.

'What you doing, Pat?' said Newman, alarmed. 'That stuff's dry as tinder. You'll have the whole tree alight!'

And he stepped forward to pull the burning brush away. Pat grabbed him by the arm, swung him round and hit him hard in the stomach. Newman went down.

'That boy needs a lesson,' he snarled. 'I'm going to roast his feet for him!'

'You'll kill him!' gasped Newman.

'I could have shot him for disobeying an order,' said Murtagh quietly, 'but I didn't. Think of this as a second chance.'

Again Rube and Newman were quelled by Murtagh's ruthless disregard for human life. Surely he had been brought in to wipe out Viall's enemies, not his own side? All three watched the flames lick the trunk of the pine, shoot up runnels of weather-hardened resin, play among the lower branches which caught, flared, crackled with new fires which rose in new hot rivers.

Hayes soon lost sight of the ground as he gained height. When he was higher than the tops of the other trees, he saw the flat plain laid out before him. Sure enough, a darker swathe led straight across it, where a rider and four led horses had flattened the grass. He yelled down with the news and began the descent.

But as he got lower, the smell of the fire got stronger. Then there was smoke that got thicker. It became so thick he couldn't breathe easily.

'Hey! Dowse the fire! Smoke's getting bad up here!'

There was no reply. He was forced to start climbing up again. When he looked down, he saw Murtagh, Rube and Newman starting off on foot along Harker's trail. Then he lost them in the smoke. But he saw Murtagh turn and stare and Hayes knew he was going to die.

There was no way down, unless he could jump to another tree. He assessed his chances. They did not look good. Hayes looked down. He saw Murtagh look back in his direction. Then he turned, caught up with the other two and walked on.

Hayes jumped.

Murtagh had abandoned his saddle at the camp. It had taken them a day to come this far on horseback. It would probably take them two to make it back on foot. Rube and Newman were carrying theirs. Soon they dropped behind, slowed by the weight. Rube made up some time after he dumped his but Newman lost further ground. Both grew footsore. Their boots got cut up on the rough stretches of the trail where sharp stones made their feet bleed.

Murtagh set a fast pace. He wanted to get back to Laureston. That was where he would find Harker. He wanted Harker like a drunk wants a drink.

Harker had not tried to cover his tracks. He left a trail as wide as a church door and as easy to follow as a candle in a dark cellar.

Around noon, Murtagh lost patience. He quickened his pace, leaving Rube to wait for Newman and both of them to find their own way home. He didn't need them. He didn't need numbers to do what Walter Viall was paying him to do.

8

Off the Leash

Billy Boden sat on his stoop, looking out. He had a clear view across gently undulating grassland that could support a sight more cattle than were grazing it now. He knew Viall had rustled some of his stock and rebranded others, but he could not prove it the way the law liked things proved. But Dick Pipes, Eddy Spence, Jake Stone, Lovell Jackson, all the men who'd been driven off their claims or forced to work for Viall, would have believed him, proof or no proof, because the self-same thing had happened to them. He swore that one day he'd see his own steers grazing his own land again, with no one able to take them away from him.

He was over the roughing up he'd been given by Viall's strong-arm boys and was feeling as good as he had in a long time. With Tom Harker riding shotgun, he reckoned he stood a real chance of saving what he had worked for and getting back what had been filched from him. Tom was the sort of man who made things happen.

Billy rolled and lit a smoke. He'd never liked the thought he was being protected by his sister. Of course, he was grateful to her for keeping Viall off him and Martha and now the baby too, though how she managed it she would never say. But now with Tom by his side, he had a feeling that things were about to change.

Even so, Billy felt uneasy. Where was Tom? He'd ridden into town yesterday morning, to stir up some support. But he hadn't come back. Had he run into a pack of Viall's men? Had he been roughed up too, or worse? Maybe he should take a ride into Laureston and find out.

He made up his mind to do just that. He stood up and was about to go in to

Martha and tell her so when his eye caught a distant movement at the edge of his pastureland. He went indoors, fetched his long glass and took a peek. He saw five horses and one rider, and that rider he'd have known in a million. He called to Martha to set the coffee pot on the stove and watched his friend all the way home.

By the time Harker slid out of the saddle at the Boden's door, the coffee was ready. When Martha asked if he was hungry and learned that he hadn't eaten all day, she quickly rustled up a dish of chow which didn't stay long on the plate.

When Harker had finished telling his tale, Billy told him the man in the green shirt, the one they called Pat, was Pat Murtagh, a professional gun. He was a fast, cold killer. Viall only called him in when somebody who was special trouble had crossed him.

'Looks like you got Viall rattled,' said Billy.

'That's what Tabitha said,' Martha chipped in.

'She was out here yesterday,' explained Billy. 'She said Walt was mad as hell after you flooded his place out. Seems he rode into town and let his boys sound off, threatening all sorts. Then Rube ran a herd clean through Jake Stone's place. Jake's dead. Viall said it was nothing to do with him, and no one could prove otherwise since there weren't any witnesses. Then he started talking about compensation for damage to his property. Sis reckons he's got out of control.'

'Did she say why?' asked Harker.

'She reckons he's putting down markers. Said he's thinking of going in for politics and won't let anything harm his reputation. There's a county election in the fall and he'll probably run for office.'

'Probably?' said Harker.

'More than that, she thought: definitely.'

Harker's mind worked on this. If Viall entered public life, he'd have to give speeches, electioneer on the hustings, be upstanding on a soapbox surrounded by crowds of voters. His picture would be in the papers. Sooner or later someone would recognize him and want him brought to book for the crimes of his past. If word got out that he'd ridden with Mundy's Marauders, he'd go nowhere except jail. If he was thinking of running for office, he must be pretty sure that even if the truth came out it wouldn't hurt him none. What did Viall have up his sleeve? Who did he have in his pocket?

'I told Tabitha that if Viall was really cutting loose,' said Harker, 'it wasn't safe for her to stay in town, but she wouldn't listen. If Viall's somehow got himself off the hook, he won't go easy on her. I'm going into Laureston and find out what's going on.'

'I'm coming with you,' said Billy. 'She's my sister and I owe her a lot. I got to take care of her.'

* * *

Lovell Jackson reined in his horse, leaned on the pommel of his saddle and drank it all in. From this spot, where the trail began the descent, he had the best view of the valley. Nowadays, like Jake Stone and the others, he ran beef for Walter Viall. His range was at the high end of Clearstream Gulch that overlooked Bluewater. Once it had been one hundred per cent his. He'd claimed it, staked it, fenced it, worked it. Then, like the others, he'd been pushed off it when Viall went on his cut-price buying spree and ended up the biggest landowner in Tate County. Now he was just a hired hand who worked for a man who knew how to get blood out of stone.

He prodded the ribs of his mount which ambled forward. Time was when he enjoyed these trips into Laureston. He'd chew the fat over a couple of beers with Jake Stone or Dick Pipes or whoever while Sam Whipple at the stores filled his order for a sack of beans, a couple of bags of flour, one of coffee and maybe a tool to replace one that was broken or worn out. But not any more. Nobody had time for it. Anyway, there wasn't much news he wanted to hear.

His horse shied, startled by the sudden appearance of a man who stepped on to the trail out of a clump of bushes. The man had a gun in his hand. He was small-made and wore a dusty, torn, green shirt.

'Get down!' he growled. 'I want your horse.'

There was no mistaking the Irish brogue nor the ice in his eyes.

Lovell did as he was told and stood without moving while the small man grabbed the reins, put one foot in the stirrup and hauled himself into the saddle. The man's scuffed boots were in an even worse state than his shirt. He pulled on the reins and went off at a lick on the Laureston road.

Lovell Jackson watched him go. It came to him that he was now further from home than he was from town. He shrugged, took another long look at the view. Then he started walking in the direction taken by the man with ice for eyes who'd stolen his horse.

★ ★ ★

The sun was setting when Harker and Billy pulled up outside the sheriff's office. They tethered their mounts and the horses Harker had taken from Viall's paid hands and which he was now returning. Rukatch stepped out on the boardwalk.

'You boys gone into the horse-flesh business?' he growled.

'No, sir,' said Harker. 'Found these broncos wandering loose. Thought I'd bring them in lest they came to some harm. If I leave them with you, whoever lost them can come and get them back whenever they want.'

News travelled fast in Laureston, where nothing happened twice an hour every day of the week.

Walter Viall was still in town. His

ranch house had been flattened and he'd moved into the hotel until his boys had fixed his place up again. The moment he heard Harker was back, he headed for the sheriff's office.

He was calmer now, but his mood was still savage. Judge Morton had gone out to Jake Stone's place personally, since a death was involved, to take a look round and establish whether or not a crime had been committed. Viall had gone with him, taking Mikey and a few of his boys who had rounded up the scattered herd. Mikey reported maybe only twenty missing. But the damage to buildings and fences was all too plain. The Judge found nothing to show how the stampede had started, which put Rube in the clear. But since there was no evidence of foul play or negligence, then Viall could hardly claim compensation for damage done to his property by his own steers. The Judge shrugged, told him it was the best he could so. He ruled that Jake's death was an accident and so was the damage. Mrs Stone took small comfort from his visit.

The decision didn't exactly please Walter Viall either. He expected better service from a judge whom he had in his pocket, bought and paid for. Nor was he satisfied by what the sheriff had to say. Rukatch had ridden out to inspect the sluice-gates above the WV spread. It sure looked like somebody had tampered with them, he said, but there was no way of telling who that person was. Could have been carelessness on the part of one of Viall's own boys or maybe an act of revenge by a disgruntled ex-employee. He also gave it as his opinion that any man who built a ranch in the run-off path of a lake had himself mainly to blame if he got washed out. That had pleased Viall even less than the Judge's ruling. No man like being called a fool.

Viall swept past the nags tethered outside the Sheriff's office and confronted Rukatch.

'How did them horses get here?' he

barked. 'One of them is Rube's. Where is he? I lost one boy, I don't intend to lose any more.'

'Tom Harker brought all four in,' said Rukatch. 'But since you're here I guess you know that.'

'Found them wandering in the hills above Bluewater,' said Harker mildly. 'No saddles on any of them. No riders neither. So I brought them in. Any man would have done the same. You don't leave a good class of stable flesh out in them parts; it's too good to be left to wolves.'

Viall was about to reply when there was a sound of hooves in the street and a murmur of voices outside. Then Pat Murtagh, dusty, breathing hard, shirt and pants torn, boots beat up beyond repair, burst through the door. He pulled up short when he saw Harker sitting relaxed on the edge of Rukatch's desk.

'Pat!' cried Viall. 'What in tarnation happened to you? Where's Rube?'

Murtagh glared at Harker. His chest

slowly stopped heaving and the fingers of his right hand, hovering on a level with the Colt in his holster, clutching at thin air. A muscle in his neck twitched. Everything about him said cold fury. But he was a man who kept a tight rein on himself. A gunslinger who couldn't master his temper didn't live long.

Turning to Viall, he said coolly: 'They told me at the hotel I'd find you here. Rube's fine. He just got held up. He'll be along presently. Tomorrow, if he walks fast, maybe the day after if he don't.' Then turning to the tall, lean man standing next to Billy Boden, he added in a low growl: 'So you're Harker.'

'Can't deny it,' said Harker coolly.

'You look plumb tuckered out, Murtagh,' said Billy. 'Horse throw you? Did you go and get yourself lost?'

Murtagh did not miss the mocking note in Billy's voice.

'You,' he said in a low, mean voice, 'got a loose mouth. But you got nothing to say, so keep your trap shut.'

Billy, who didn't scare any easier than Harker, smiled back. 'No need to get riled, friend,' he said. 'Had you down for a natty dresser, though.'

'It's been a long day, Pat,' said Viall diplomatically, 'let's go and get you cleaned up. Something to eat and a change of clothes will make all the difference. Maybe Rube's shown up there by now.'

Murtagh caught his boss's eye. There was no sense in starting anything with the sheriff looking on. So he pushed his hat on to the back of his head and said, 'Sure thing. Lead on.'

Then without a backward glance he and Viall, plus three of Viall's boys, walked a way down the street to Ma Kelly's. Murtagh never drank when he was on a job. He ordered a pot of coffee and a plate of her corned beef hash.

'What happened up there in the mountains, Pat?' asked Viall. 'Harker jump you?'

Murtagh told the tale, however, he toned it down. But it still left him looking foolish. Enzo Taparo, one of Viall's drovers smiled. Another, Newt Thornton, sniggered openly.

'You think that's funny, boy?' snapped Murtagh and without waiting for an answer, he flung the contents of the coffee pot at his head. Thornton leaped to his feet, clawing at his face, howling and saying how he couldn't see, how he was blinded. Then Murtagh was on him. A left to the body brought his arms down and a right caught him over the ear. Newt Thornton went down and sure looked like he wasn't going to get up again till next week. But Murtagh wasn't done with him. He waded in with his boots which, though beat up, landed with sickening regularity on Harris's arms, belly, head until Viall yanked hard on one of his arms and pulled him off.

'Cut it out, Pat! You'll kill him!'

Murtagh paused, blowing hard. Then he sat down again while Enzo and Viall lifted Thornton on to a chair and called for hot water and towels to clean him up.

'Jees, Pat,' said Viall. 'What you do that for? Newt's on our side!'

'No one laughs at me,' said Pat savagely.

'Well, in future, keep it for Harker. Don't be a fool, man! When my business is finished, you can spread his carcase all across the Rocky Mountains for all I care. But until then I don't want you putting any more of my boys in bed, you comprendo? If not, you can get out now!'

Pat Murtagh looked him in the eye and what he saw sobered him up. He'd known Walt from way back, from the days when both of them had ridden with Mundy. He knew what Walt was made of, he'd seen him in action. Pat feared no man. But if he did, Walter Viall would be top of the list.

He nodded, then he put Walt out of his mind and smiled. He felt better, thinking how much he'd enjoy spreading Harker over those rugged Rockies.

Enzo saw the look on his face. He didn't like it.

Abe Monkman also hurried across to Rukatch's office the moment he heard Harker was back. He listened to the story and felt his spirits rise.

'What have you got on Murtagh?' asked Harker.

'Not much. The word is he came over from Ireland as a boy, during the famine. Always wears a green shirt in honour of the old country. Never stays any place long. Keeps on the move. Works for whoever pays best. If we offered him more than Viall, he'd come over to us.'

'I doubt it,' said Billy with a grin. 'Tom's got under his skin. I don't think he'd want to work with us.'

'I'd need to check this, but from what I recollect he must have killed at least a dozen men. He's fast, but he avoids face-to-face stand-offs. Most of the men he's killed went to meet their maker with a look of surprise on their mugs or holes in their backs. But he gets results. So people like Viall keep hiring him.'

'Until these last few days,' said Harker, 'Tabitha has managed to keep him on a leash. What's happened recently to change that?'

Abe hesitated a moment then shrugged his shoulders: 'Walt's going on the rampage, so I guess there's no point in keeping it quiet any more. Some of you know anyway. Viall was one of Mundy's Marauders and Tabitha can prove it.'

Sheriff Rukatch gave a whistle of surprise. 'If that had got out, he'd now be staring at the sky through bars,' he said.

'But soon it won't matter if he stands on a street corner and sings 'I once rode with Mundy and I still don't give a damn' to the tune of John Brown's Body. The politicians back east are going to vote an amnesty for all the wrong things that were done in the War. There's plenty want to let bygones be bygones. And they have a point. If the Union goes after every fool that forgot his manners when he had a tunic on his back and gun in his hand, scores would go on being settled until the end of time and we'd never have peace. Start a fresh page, they say, forget the old battles and work together to fix the new problems. There's a lot to be said for it.'

'So even if Walt does decide to run for public office and gets his picture in the paper,' said Billy, 'it won't matter if he's recognized. He'll just say sorry and promise to serve the people with heart and soul. He's off the hook. There'll be no holding him now.'

A grim silence filled the sheriff's office.

'Best we can hope for is that he'll get overconfident and trip himself up.'

'Oh, I think we can do a mite better than that,' said Harker with a grin.

All four drifted across to the hotel where they continued the discussion.

'I'd say we've got a fight on our hands,' said Rukatch. 'Viall's got over thirty men, plus his two sons, Mikey and Rube, and Murtagh. How many can we muster?'

Billy and Abe did a quick count and came up with fifteen names at the outside.

'The first thing we do is reduce the odds,' said Harker, 'and the second is to go on the offensive. I'm not planning to sit around and wait for things to happen.'

While they tossed around ideas for making things happen, Abe went to the counter of the bar for beers. When he got back, he was excited.

'Seems there's been trouble at Ma Kelly's. One of Viall's boys said or did something, I didn't catch what, that made Murtagh mad. Threw boiling coffee in his face then laid into him with his boots. If Viall hadn't pulled him off, he'd have killed him. The drover who told me, Enzo, sounded real scared. He reckoned nobody was safe from Murtagh. He doesn't hurt people just for the money: he does it because he likes it. Enzo said he wasn't going to stick around and get beaten up or killed by Viall's hired gun. Some of the other boys there thought the same way.'

'Sounds like Murtagh is reducing the odds for us,' said Billy.

'From what they said,' said Abe, 'I got the impression there's bad feeling in Viall's camp. His boys said they hadn't been paid for a month. Enzo said he was going to rustle a couple of hundred head of Viall's stock and drive them over to Acre Creek and sell them in lieu of pay.'

'The rats are deserting the ship,' said Billy with a grin. 'Looks like Viall and Murtagh are doing our job for us.'

But before anyone could start thinking the job was almost done, Lovell Jackson, covered in dust, grey with exhaustion, walked in through the door.

'They said in the hotel I'd find you here, Billy. I got a message for you. They got your wife. You have to go and sign a paper saying you give up your claim on Bluewater. Then they'll give her back to you. If you don't . . . '

9

Fightback

Billy was on his feet, his face suddenly ashen, knuckles showing white.

'Who gave you the message, Lovell? Where have they got Martha? Did you see her? Is she all right?'

They sat Lovell down. He told them how, after the man in the green shirt had stolen his horse, he'd had to walk to Laureston. He'd reached the fork in the road near the Acre Creek turn-off when he'd been overtaken by Mikey and Rube Viall. They'd circled him, Indian fashion, and made threats.

'They said to get myself into Laureston, find you and pass on what I just told you, about holding Martha and how you was to sign their paper.'

'Did they say where they were holding her?' said Billy?

'Nope,' said Lovell. 'You got to ride out to where they stopped me, which was by the bridge near where Frank Dakins had his claim. They'll be waiting for you. Then they let me go so I could deliver the message. When I was out of range I snitched a look or two over my shoulder. I ain't exactly sure, but I reckon they must have headed off the road up towards the old Dakins place. Couldn't have gone anywhere else.'

'That's Frank Dakins's old place,' explained Abe, 'couple of miles out on the Acre Creek road. Viall bought it the same way he bought everybody else's. He built himself a cabin on the property a year or two back. Could well be that's where she's at.'

'Did you see any more of Viall's men?' asked Billy.

'They was just the two of them, Mikey and Rube, like I said. Rube looked as if he'd been dragged through a hedge. But both of them acted mighty pleased with themselves. Like the cat that's had the cream.'

'Thanks, Lovell,' said Billy. 'Sorry you got mixed up in this.'

'No thanks required, Billy, you can always count on me. I don't take kindly to having my horse taken off me. And I don't like men with guns telling me what to do, neither.'

'Good to know you're with us, Lovell,' said Billy. 'We'll talk later. But now I got to go and get Martha. You coming, Tom? I'll get the horses,' he added, anxious to be gone.

Harker felt his anger rise. He'd had a bellyful of Viall throwing his weight around. The first job was to mobilize the support everybody kept talking about. It was time for actions, not promises. He quickly outlined his plan. The Sheriff, Lovell, Abe and maybe Tabitha, if she was game, would ride round the homesteads and raise as many men who were prepared to fight Viall for control of Laureston.

★ ★ ★

The moon was up now and it turned the trail bluey-white and silver. As they rode, Billy gave Harker all he knew about Dakins.

'He was a loner, raised a few crops, not a cattleman. He'd lost an arm somewhere along the way and folks reckoned that's what made him so ornery. He arrived here from back east around the same time as most of the others and staked a claim just like everybody did. But he was never a sociable man. When Viall started expanding, old Dakins was the first to sell up, or so folks said. No one knew for sure, but one day somebody noticed that the cantankerous old buzzard hadn't been around for a while. Nor did he ever show up again. But Viall had a bill of sale, all signed and legal. He built a log cabin out there, with a stone chimney. He uses it for a hunting lodge.'

They slowed as they approached the fork where Lovell had been stopped. The road to Acre Creek peeled off just

168

after a stone bridge. When they reached the bridge, Mikey Viall stepped out from a growth of bushes.

'Get off the horse,' he said. 'I mean just you, Billy boy. Your friend can turn round and go back the way he came. He got no business here. All you got to do is sign a paper, collect your lady and you'll be free to go, all as quick as Jack Flash and quiet as an egg.'

Billy did what he was told. He dismounted and held his horse's rein and waited. Neither he nor Harker even thought of making an argument of it. This was no time for shoot-outs. Then Rube Viall emerged from behind a shoulder of rock. He had a carbine too. He cradled it comfortably in his arms.

'You heard my brother,' he said to Harker. 'Get your hide out of my sight. Now!'

Without a word, Harker wheeled his horse and cantered back along the road he'd just ridden. When he'd gone a quarter of a mile, he stopped and looked back. The three men, dark splashes in a silver landscape, hadn't moved. Then Rube raised his carbine and loosed off a shot. The range was too great for it to be meant seriously. It was a warning. Duly warned, Harker went on his way, rounded a bend and lost sight of the Viall brothers and his old friend.

All the while, he'd been thinking. Most likely, Mikey and Rube would have left a guard on Martha and probably they'd have other men with them for support, which made maybe five or six guns, all told. He knew they'd never let Billy and Martha go once the paper was signed. He could count on Billy to stall, but he knew he had to get to the lodge before it was too late. Sure, Billy could look after himself. But one man against maybe half a dozen was a bet too far.

He swung off the trail and worked his way back until he guessed he was about level with the bridge and maybe forty yards downwind of it. He dismounted, tethered his horse to a moon-silvered bush, made some ground on foot, climbed a rock and took a peek. Billy and Mikey were gone but Rube was still there, guarding the bridge.

Harker made another hundred yards, took another sighting. Rube was still on the bridge. His back was turned. Harker dodged across the road at a low run and ducked into cover. He waited to find out if Rube had heard him, but no shot came. Using all his field craft, he moved quickly and silently, eyes and ears open for look-outs posted along the way. He followed a line parallel to the trail that led up to the Dakins place. He'd gone half a mile when he was suddenly stopped in his tracks. A match flared not twenty yards upwind to his left. Moving like a cat, he put distance between himself and the careless sentry.

He now crossed an area of broken boulders which threw deep shadows. Here the going was trickier. Several times he tripped over rocks or roots which he could not see and made more noise than he wanted to. But he stayed parallel to the trail and made good progress towards the cabin. He walked blindly into a thicket of bushes growing in the ebony-black shadow of a rock that looked like a pyramid, lost his footing and next moment was falling. The crevasse was no more than fifteen feet deep. But the drop was enough to wind him and leave him stunned and wondering if he'd broken anything.

Although the rim of the crevasse was overgrown by thick brush, it was open to the sky and the moon shone down brightly into it, illuminating the floor which was covered with leaves, stones and debris of many seasons.

Harker tried out his arms and legs. Nothing hurt enough to suggest anything was broken. Apart from the blow to his pride for doing such a tom-fool thing as fall down a hole, he'd come to no harm. He glanced around him, looking for the quickest way up and out of there. He wasn't doing Billy any good down a hole and there was no time to waste.

The sides of the pit were a mite off vertical. But there were enough projecting rocks and exposed roots to provide plenty of footholds. He sat up, stretched and found himself staring at a grinning skull.

It was part of a skeleton which had been there a long time. It lay on its back. Summer heat and winter rain had left little but bones. The flesh had gone, leaving just a bleached skeleton with strips of dry, leathery skin still attached here and there to the bones. Shreds of denim pants were stuck to the legs and tatters of what looked like a checked shirt clung to the ribcage. One leg was broken and twisted under the torso.

He reckoned the man had come to grief the same way he had — at night when it was too dark or too wild to see, or maybe he was plain drunk — but had come off a lot worse. Harker had a bump on his head which was swelling quickly. But with a leg so badly broken, the man could never have even tried to climb out. A terrible death.

Then Harker stiffened. He was wrong. In the middle of the skull's forehead was a round hole about the size of a slug from a Colt. The man hadn't died a lingering death at all: he'd been shot in the head. He must have been already dead when he'd been thrown into the crevasse which had turned into his grave. Harker noticed something else.

The corpse's good leg was straight out and partly buried under dried leaves. But one arm was invisible too, though it wasn't because it was buried under leaves but because it wasn't there. It had never been there. Harker suddenly knew that he was looking at the mortal remains of one-armed Frank Dakins, as lonesome in death as he had been in life.

He got to his knees for a closer look and saw, nestling among the bones of the ribcage, a six-shooter, a well-rusted Colt. It couldn't have belonged to Dakins for there was no sign of a belt and holster. It must have been dropped or thrown down by the killer after he'd tipped the body into the hole, to get rid of it. Harker picked it up. There were notches on the butt. He held it up, holding it this way and that to make the most of the pale light. Seen from a certain angle, the notches said WV.

Walter Viall!

Then Harker knew what had happened. Dakins had been shot through the head. Viall might have a bill of sale to show the land was his, but Frank Dakins had not signed it, at least not of his own free will. He had been murdered by the only person likely to benefit from his death. Viall had got his hands on the Dakins outfit by signing the contract of sale with his six-gun. And here was proof, the kind lawyers liked: the gun, found so near the body, would send Walter Viall to the gallows. No fancy connections with politicians in the state legislature, no amount of amnesties voted back east would get Viall off a charge of murder.

But all that was for tomorrow. Just

now, he had something else to take care of.

He put the gun back where he'd found it, stood up, dusted himself off, and climbed out of the hole. The moon was still high and he continued negotiating a way through rock and shadow. Then there was a light fifty yards to his left. It came from a window in a cabin which could well be a hunting lodge.

It was sturdy, one-storey and log-built in the old style. It stood on a low elevation against a wood of deep black ponderosa pine. It had a shallow-sloped roof and was a good size. An area had been cleared in front of the house to provide a view. A well-tended cinder track led up to the front door and ran all the way round the property, connecting with a couple of outbuildings which Harker guessed were stables and storehouses. There was no wind, but he could hear no sound from the house.

Keeping his head down, he ran across

the exposed front area, staying low, jumped the path to avoid crunching the cinders and stopped when he'd reached the side of the house with the lighted window he had seen. He crept along until he reached the window and risked a look. An oil lamp hung from a beam. It showed Billy in a chair with his hands tied behind his back, two men Harker had never seen before, and Mikey who was bunching his fist. On a table was a sheet of paper, ink in a bottle and a pen. Harker heard him say something but couldn't catch the words. He didn't have to; he could guess what he said when Billy shook his head. Mikey punched him high on his right temple, then repeated what he'd said before. Then he hit Billy when he shook his head again. Billy's face was red, his eyes swollen and his mouth was bloody. Harker thought: 'Here we go again!'

He ducked under the window and moved to the rear of the cabin. Through a window with secure bars across it, he saw Martha. She was alone. He tapped lightly on the glass. She looked up and he saw relief in her eyes. He put a finger to his lips then crept along the wall until he found a door. He listened but heard nothing. He tried the latch. It lifted soundlessly and then he was in and facing a man — that made six in all, Harker reckoned, including the two Viall brothers — who was pointing a gun at him.

'What you want, stranger?' the man growled in a voice that seemed to come from his boots.

'Just passing by,' said Harker. 'I'm lost. I reckoned I could get some directions — '

He was interrupted by a woman's scream. The man with the gun half turned to see what was going on. Harker was on him at once and felled him with a crashing right to the jaw. The man went down and did not get up. Harker kicked his gun away, moved quickly to the door of the room holding Martha, turned the key in the lock and she stepped out.

'I heard voices,' she whispered. 'I reckoned you'd run into trouble. I thought hollering might help.'

'You hollered just fine,' said Harker with a grin. 'It put the man off his stroke a treat.'

'They've got Billy,' said Martha worriedly, 'and they're hurting him.'

'I know. I'll just go get him for you.'

Down the corridor a door opened and a voice called, 'What was that row, Spence? Need any help?'

'Nope. All fine,' growled Harker in a deep, gravelly growl which fooled the man down the corridor who went back in and shut the door behind him.

'Get something to tie up our friend here,' said Harker. 'We don't want him coming round and giving trouble.'

Leaving Martha to it, he turned and walked noiselessly along the corridor to the room where Billy was being roughed up. He raised his right leg and prepared to kick the door down. Then he thought better of it, lifted the latch and was inside with a gun in his fist before anyone knew he was there. Without raising a sweat, Harker had got the drop on Mikey and his two sidekicks. They froze.

It was Billy who broke the silence.

'What kept you, Tom?' he said indistinctly through broken lips.

'Isn't it time you stopped letting Viall's boys take advantage of you?' Harker grinned back.

He ordered Mikey and his boys to the end of the room and told them to stand facing the wall. He kept them covered with the Colt and with his free hand untied Billy. Billy rubbed his wrists to restore the circulation and wiped most of the blood off his mouth with the sleeve of his shirt.

'Get their guns, Billy,' said Harker, 'while I keep them covered.'

Billy stuck Mikey's six-shooter in his belt and tossed the other men's guns into the dead ashes in the chimney place. As he did so, Martha walked in. Both Harker and Billy looked up. Mikey made the most of his chance.

He swung round and aimed a right at Billy. Billy had already soaked up a lot of punishment and wasn't quick enough to avoid his fist entirely. But he ducked low enough to turn the punch into a blow that glanced off the top of his head. Then he moved into the crouch which Harker remembered from the old days. He stuck a left in Mikey's face and a right to the ribs which pushed him back. Stalking his man, he followed up with a combination of lefts and rights which cut Mikey's face to ribbons. A sweet cross opened a two-inch split in his cheek and a straight left loosened some teeth. Then Billy switched to Mikey's body. A solid shot to the heart made him gasp and a sledgehammer to the solar plexus took his wind and landed him on the seat of his pants on the plank floor.

'Get up!' said Billy. 'You're good at dishing it out. Let's see how good you are at taking it!'

He didn't seem to be breathing any harder, but Mikey stayed where he was.

He'd had enough.

'Pick him up,' said Harker to Mikey's boys who'd been about as much use to him as a hole in a bucket, 'and tie his hands.'

He herded both men into the room with the window bars and then fetched the still unconscious body of the guard Martha had trussed up like a prize turkey. He shut the door on them and locked it. He didn't want them going anywhere. They were witnesses. They could testify that Viall used strong-arm tactics, including abduction and violence, to get his way. They were proof, the kind of living, talking proof that lawyers liked.

'Mikey comes with us,' said Harker. 'And we'll take Rube too. It'll knock Viall's eye out seeing both of them behind bars. Because that's where they're going.'

'Of course,' said Billy, remembering. 'Rube's still down by the bridge.'

'And there's also a look-out to take care of half way down the trail,' said

Harker. 'We ain't done yet, Billy-boy.'

Leaving Martha pointing a gun at Mikey who was gagged and tied to a chair, Harker and Billy moved off silently down the hill.

It was like the old days, just before the Battle of Nashville, when they'd been detailed to scout out no-man's-land. They located the look-out, who was asleep and snoring. They took him back to the house and dumped him in the barred cell with the others. Then Martha picked out mounts from the stable and, with Mikey tied to his nag, they walked their horses down the trail, making no noise. They halted fifty yards from the bridge. Harker left Billy and Martha to keep Mikey quiet while he went to collect Rube, who was sitting on a rock.

The first Rube knew anything was wrong was when he felt the barrel of a gun rammed into his left kidney. Startled, he dropped his carbine, turned to find out what was happening and placed his jaw in the path of Harker's fist. His head was suddenly full of stars and bright whirling pinwheels.

When he woke up, he was sitting on his horse, with his hands tied behind his back and a rope strapping his feet under its belly. He glanced to his left and saw Mikey, also trussed up, his face battered and somehow rearranged, ambling alongside. He heard unhurried hoofs behind him.

'What's going on?' he asked. 'Where we going?'

'Jail,' said a voice he knew.

Harker! He cursed himself for a fool. He should have shot him when he'd had the chance.

The moon had set. But the night was already fading in the east. Another day was dawning and the squeeze was being put on Walter Viall's past, present and future.

10

Stampede

Sheriff Rukatch was sitting in his chair in his office. He wasn't alone. On the other side of his desk Tabitha and Walt Viall faced each other.

'They wrecked the place,' said Tabitha, her fists clenched in anger. 'And even before they got drunk on my liquor not one of them paid for a single drink. They never intended to.'

There'd been another rumpus. More of Viall's men had ridden into town late the previous night and whooped it up. They'd had themselves a whale of a time in the hotel. By the time the last man standing had fallen down, the place was a mess. The windows had been smashed, the chandelier hadn't taken kindly to being swung on, doors had been wrenched off their hinges, the barkeep was nursing a broken jaw, there was broken glass everywhere and only one chair in the whole place still had four legs.

'Don't see how it's any of my business what the boys get up to in their own time,' drawled Walter Viall. 'They work hard. It ain't a surprise if they play hard too. It's the sort of thing you got to expect in your line of business, ma'am. You should think yourself lucky no one burned the place down.'

'Don't sound like the usual class of ructions to me,' said Rukatch. 'Seems like it all got out of hand.'

'You could have stopped it, Walt, but you didn't,' said Tabitha. 'They couldn't have behaved any worse if you'd told them to smash the place up and put me out of business. Is that what you want?'

Viall narrowed his eyes: 'Is that an accusation? If so, I hope you got evidence that would stand up in a court of law.'

'You don't fool me,' said Tabitha.

'You're softening Laureston up. You want everybody to know no one can stop you doing whatever you want here. And what you want is to take over the whole town.'

She stopped. Outside there was a sound of horses' hoofs, a murmur of voices and then of boots on the boardwalk. The door opened.

'Morning, Sheriff,' said Tom Harker. 'You're up and about early. And I see you got company too. But I guess you'll find room for a couple more inside . . .'

Behind him, Billy Boden steered Mikey and Rube with the muzzle of Rube's carbine. Both had their hands tied behind their backs.

' . . . but they'll need a cell to cool off in,' said Harker.

'What's the meaning of this?' said Viall, getting to his feet. 'What do you think you're doing? Untie my boys!'

'No can do,' said Harker. 'These two have been up to no good.'

'Release them!' barked Walt.

'No sir, they've been real bad boys.

187

They've done real bad things.'

'Such as?' said Walt.

'Try abduction, extortion, threats with violence, actual violence,' said Billy. 'Sheriff, lock 'em up.'

'Can you make those charges stick?' asked Rukatch.

'Sure. We got all the witnesses the law could want,' said Billy, 'not to mention my bust lip and swollen cheek here.'

Then Martha told the Sheriff how she'd been kept a prisoner in Walter Viall's hunting lodge and how Billy had been beaten up because he wouldn't sign his property away. It was enough evidence to be going on with.

'You admit doing these things, boys?' Rukatch asked.

'What if we do,' grinned Rube.

'Ain't nobody can stop us,' said Mikey, 'ain't your jail going to hold us.'

'That's damn right,' snarled Viall. 'You won't get away with this, Harker. I'm going round to see Judge Morton and get my boys sprung. I'll be back!'

Rukatch locked Mikey and Rube in

the cells. It didn't take long and he was back in time to hear Billy telling Tabitha how he and Tom Harker had freed Martha and put four of Viall's men out of action, not to mention his two sons. Then she told him how Viall had stood by while a dozen or so of his boys had run amok in the hotel. To her surprise, Harker said he was glad to hear it.

'Means they're still hung over and easy meat. Let's get over there now and neutralize some more of Walt's troops.'

The hotel looked as if a tornado had come in through the front door and gone out the back. Debris and shards of glass littered the floor and here and there lay the bodies of still boozed-up, snoring cowhands. Harker, Billy and the sheriff went among them and relieved them of their guns. One by one the sleepers woke up, held their heads and stared blearily around them. The sheriff offered them a choice: go to jail for wrecking the place or make a voluntary contribution to a fund to repair the damage. They asked how much? The sheriff said all you got. They emptied their pockets into his hat.

'Now get out of town,' he said.

'What about our guns?'

'You're cowhands, not gunslingers. Cowhands don't need six-shooters. Now get out of my town!'

They went.

Not long after they'd gone, Walt Viall rode fast down the main street, raising dust, and headed out towards his ranch without stopping by the sheriff's office.

'Looks like the judge didn't come across with that order for the release of his boys,' said Rukatch. 'But Walt will be back. He's got no choice. If he takes this lying down, he'll be finished in Laureston. Nobody would take him seriously any more.'

While they were eating a makeshift breakfast rustled up by Tabitha and Martha in the wrecked kitchen, Harker told how he'd found Walter Viall's rusted Colt next to Frank Dakins's dead body.

'Today we make our move,' he said.

'But however it turns out Walt will have to answer some awkward questions.'

'If what you say is true, there's more than enough there to put him away for good,' said Rukatch thoughtfully.

'It's true all right. The hole Frank's in is in some bushes, half way up the trail, near a rock shaped like a pyramid. There's no doubt. We've got him cold. He might be able to wriggle out of his connections with Mundy, but not a charge of murder.'

Abe Monkman breezed in. He took one look at the destruction and whistled.

'What happened?' he said. 'Sky fall on the place?'

They found a plate for him and while he ate he told them the final tally: thirteen guns on side, thirteen good men who'd had enough of having their lives ruled by Viall. He'd called them to a meeting for noon, a council of war, by the cottonwoods in Breakjaw Creek just outside town. Harker grunted and said until then he needed to do some thinking. He found a quiet spot, put his feet up, tipped his hat over his eyes and promptly went to sleep.

★ ★ ★

Walter Viall rode back to the ranch filled with cold fury. Things weren't going to plan. First, Judge Morton had turned him down, saying he'd have to hear the evidence before he could hand out orders for the release of Mikey and Rube. He was getting cautious. He'd bent a good few rules for Walt in his time but he wasn't going to take any more chances, not with elections coming up. Viall could no longer count on having him on side.

Then there was the plain fact that Walt was losing men. Hayes, who had lived to tell the tale, had told it and a lot of the hands hadn't liked what they heard. But Hayes had done more than talk. He had joined up with Newman and Enzo and together they'd rustled a couple of hundred head of cattle from

192

the outlying ranges. Said it was back pay. The idea could be catching, especially since Viall couldn't spare men to go chasing after them.

He had to stop the rot fast, show his boys, Harker and the townspeople that he still called the shots. Then something he had said to Tabitha came back to him about being grateful that no one had burned the hotel down. But that didn't mean it couldn't happen, nor rule out it happening to a bank or a church or a newspaper office. A blaze would put his mark on the town, show people he couldn't be stopped.

After the flood, he'd called in as many cowhands from the outlying grasslands as he could spare without letting steers wander off and get lost. He'd set them to work rebuilding the ranch. As he turned off the trail to it, he saw that fences had already been repaired and the main house had a roof again and the walls of most of the outbuildings were already six feet high.

From the new porch, which smelled

of fresh pine, Pat Murtagh, in a freshly laundered green shirt, watched him ride up. He reached for the bottle standing next to his coffee cup and poured a stiff drink in a spare glass. Viall swung down off his horse, tethered it and perched on the hitching rail. The drink hardly touched the sides. He poured himself another. Only then did Murtagh speak.

'Seems you're letting the competition get ahead of you, Walt. What was it Mundy used to say when the boys started grumbling that their pockets were flapping empty?'

'He used to say 'there's muttering in the ranks tonight',' said Viall.

'Well, Walt, there's plenty who're muttering in your ranks. You better do something about it.'

'Don't worry,' said Viall grimly, 'it's all in hand. Tell the men to knock off and get some rest. It's going to be a busy night.'

★ ★ ★

The noon meeting went well. Thirteen men, all armed and ready for a showdown, turned up. That made about seventeen guns in all, eighteen if you counted Doc Prentice who'd arrived carrying an aged long-barrelled, one-shot pistol he said was his father's and didn't look as if it had been fired since the war with Spain. Harker would have liked more but the turnout was better than he'd expected. Together, they mapped out a plan of campaign. They agreed that as a small force they would be more effective concentrated in one place than spread out. Harker detailed half a dozen men to see what they could do to defend the town. The first thing was to get people off the streets and over to Breakjaw Creek where they'd be far enough away from the shooting-match to be safe. He detailed Doc Prentice to organize it, and persuaded Martha and Tabitha they would be more use there than in the direct firing line in Laureston.

Meanwhile, there were windows to

be boarded up, streets cleared, sniper points to fortify on the roof of the hotel and the Church, which both commanded clear lines of fire. The strongest building was Whipple's store. It was also the oldest, the original staging post, built of stone, with small windows. It had resisted every Indian attack ever mounted to take it. Harker left Abe to oversee the work while he took the rest of the men out along the Santa Fe road where there was a diversion to organize.

At intervals, two or three men peeled off the bunch and struck out across the range with orders to round up all the WV-branded stock they could find and drive them to a shallow valley a couple of miles west of Walter Viall's ranch.

Harker did not go with the last team on herding duty but rode up to the lake at the back of Viall's spread. Keeping his head down to avoid being skylined, he found a vantage point and looked down. A lot of the damage from his flood had been repaired and there was an organized air to the place. Men were walking around purposefully, carrying buckets and tools and lengths of timber. Others stood on ladders, nailed slats on roofs and mixed mortar. Saddle-horses grazed in newly fenced paddocks. He saw a green shirt.

He stood up, still keeping his head low, and turned to go back to his horse. As he did so, he almost trod on an old man who had been snoozing in the grass. The man sat up. He looked scared.

'You're Harker,' he said. 'You're the one damn near drownded me, Viall and all his boys. That was some trick!'

'You work for Walt?'

'Sure thing. Jedediah Parsons is the name. But they all call me Cookie on account of me being of no account and chief and only cook.'

'What are you doing up here, Jed? How come you're not down there cooking?'

'I gave 'em beef stew and taters around noon, and that's me finished for today. There's nothing to do because there'll be no chow served tonight. Special orders. The boss said all hands is going into town around sundown. Something big going to happen.'

'What sort of thing, Jed?'

'He didn't say. But everybody was to take a gun, so I guess it's not a Sunday School party. Are you going to kill me now?'

'Why would I do that, Jed? I got nothing against you. I never tasted your cooking.'

Jedediah grinned.

'It ain't that bad, though to be fair, I get complaints. But look here, Mr Harker, what you doing here? They said you was trouble. You going to play that sluice trick again?'

'Nope. But if I was you, I'd stay up here enjoying the sunshine for as long as it lasts. I wouldn't go down to the ranch. It's going to be a lot healthier here. You'll have a grandstand view.'

'Of what?' asked Jedediah.

But Harker was already striding

through the grass towards his horse.

When he reached the wide, shallow valley where his men were to meet up with the WV steers, it was full of cattle and more were being driven to join them. There must have been a couple of thousand in all.

'Is that the end of them?' he asked.

'We didn't roust out every last one,' said Lovell. 'Wasn't enough time. But we got enough. All the boys are here. When are you figuring to let 'em go?'

'Just as soon as we've settled a few details.'

Harker called the riders together and said who was to ride on the herd's right flank, who on the left, and who would bring up the rear. They took up their positions. When they were all ready, he joined the drovers at the back. For a moment he remained perfectly still. Then he let go an almighty whoop and fired three shots in the air. The steers nearest to him jittered nervously, showed the whites of their eyes and then pushed into the rumps of the steers in front of them. The riders on the flanks hollered, cracked whips, fired over the heads of the herd and made as much noise as they could. Soon the movement which had begun at the rear and on both sides of the heaving mass of cattle spread to other parts, like oil over rocks. The pace quickened, individual animals were lost in the mass and the whole herd began to move forward like some unstoppable flow of mud.

In minutes, the wide shallow valley which had held them was empty again. Above it, the dust raised by the hoofs of thousands of cattle began to fall back down to earth.

Harker and his men drove them on from the back while the side riders steered them due east, over the flat grazing lands, stopping them turning or spreading out too far. Nothing could halt them now. The air was filled with the pounding of hoofs on hard turf and the ground trembled under the wild advance of so many tons of prime beef.

Fences were carried away. A stand of pine on a low hill vanished as it was engulfed. When the black tide had passed on, all that was left was matchwood.

But the stampede was still under control. Riders drove their horses among the panting steers, nudging them into line, urging them on, stopping them breaking away. From the back, Harker looked up. Above him rose the rim of the plateau where it began a slow descent to Viall's ranch. He waited a moment longer then fired three times in the air.

It was the prearranged signal to disengage. The riders in the rear dropped back. Those on each wing went wide, putting clear ground between them and the charging beasts before swinging back and joining the group bringing up the rear. From a safe distance they watched the stampede race on in front of them. The thunder grew less loud, the ground stopped shuddering, the dust began to settle and through it finally Harker saw that the Viall spread had been flattened for a second time. The neat fences, the ranch house, the barn walls were all gone.

The men who had been working on the site had heard the cattle pouring down on them and had got out on their horses before they too went the way of everything that stood in its path. When the stampede had passed, they set off in pursuit, to halt them before too many were lost. But the galloping mass roared on, showing no sign of stopping.

'They'll have their work cut out,' said Lovell Jackson with satisfaction. 'Them steers will run and run until they find water or decide they've had enough.'

'That's exactly what I had in mind,' grinned Harker. 'That's a lot of money on legs you see there running over hill and dale. Viall can't afford to let them steers go. He'll have to commit men to the pursuit. That means fewer guns to take into Laureston. Come on,' he said, wheeling his horse, 'time to get back.'

A quarter of a mile below, Walter Viall

stood in the midst of the wreckage for the second time in a few days. He looked up, his eye caught by a movement, and saw Harker and his men head off over the crest of the hill back towards town.

He too was thinking about how the odds had changed. A score of hands who'd gone after his steers meant a score fewer guns to fight his battles for him. His face was white with anger. Harker had stolen another march on him, tied his hands. He called up his remaining men and ordered them to follow him.

11

Battle is Joined

Pat Murtagh led his horse out of a clump of pinewoods where the WV ranch's trail met the Santa Fe road. Viall held up a hand and the troop came to a halt. Murtagh rode into its midst. That helped even up those odds some, thought Viall.

'This whole thing sure looks like a bucket of pigswill to me, Walt,' he said, with a curl of the lip. 'You said it would be a pushover. Just take Harker out and the rest of town would roll over, like puppy dogs. But it ain't working out like that.'

'I don't remember as how you've earned your keep neither,' snapped Viall. 'Harker had no problem giving you the runaround. He messed up one of your nice shirts and then made you look a fool in the sheriff's office.'

Murtagh's face darkened with anger. Viall held up one hand.

'But there ain't no sense falling out, Pat. We always worked as a team. I admit it: I underestimated Harker. But I got his measure now. There'll be no more mistakes. Are you still on board?'

Murtagh hesitated a moment then relaxed.

'Sure,' he smiled. 'Why not? I fancy putting a slug in his hide. Harker's an irritation.'

Viall counted the hands who'd gathered around. Twenty-seven. It should be enough. But not all were armed.

'Where are your guns?' he barked.

'The sheriff and that new man, Harker, they took them off us,' said Perce Rogers, the burly foreman, 'in the hotel. Wasn't our fault. We was sleeping it off at the time.'

'You goddam idiots!' shouted Viall. 'I don't pay you to get so drunk you can't look after yourselves or your weapons!'

'You haven't paid us at all for weeks, boss,' said Perce. 'The boys wanted me to speak to you about it.'

'You'll get your money. Now tell me, where'd they put the guns?'

'Took them to the sheriff's office, I guess,' said Perce.

'That's where we're going. They got Mikey and Rube there too. When we've sprung them, you'll get your guns. And when we've got your guns, you can shoot the place up, even rob the bank if you've a mind to it. Think of it as a bonus. Ain't nobody going to stop us doing exactly what we want. Laureston is ours for the taking.'

'Now just hold on a sec, Mr Viall' said Perce. 'We're cowhands. Mayhem of a Saturday night is one thing. But springing prisoners, robbing banks, well, it ain't what we signed on for and if you ask — '

He got no further. There was a shot, a red flower blossomed over his heart and he slid from the saddle on to the trail.

Murtagh waved his six-shooter at the crowd.

'Anybody else got something to say?' said Pat. 'No? Then let's do what Mr Viall said. Let's ride!'

He fired in the air and, like the steers they were used to driving, the men took off fast down the trail towards Laureston. Murtagh brought up the rear. He wasn't counting on letting any deserters drop off the back of the pack.

They rode through Laureston unopposed. The streets were still and empty. Viall expected nothing else: the whole town must know there was no sense in trying to fight back and he guessed everybody thought it best to hibernate for a while.

He swung down outside the sheriff's office, drew his gun, ordered a couple of his armed boys to follow, ran up the steps and kicked the door open. There was no one inside. There was no one in the cells either. He called for Mikey and Rube but there was no reply. He told one of his men to shoot the lock off the door of the cupboard where Rukatch stored lost or stolen or confiscated property. There were no guns inside. Then he heard a shot. It came from his left, a way up the street.

When he got outside, his men had scattered and taken cover. He joined Murtagh behind a buckboard.

'Sniper,' said Pat. 'Looks like it came from the hotel. Did you get the guns?'

'No, nor my two boys neither,' snarled Viall.

'Looks like we walked into a trap. Harker's outsmarted you again, compadre. They've got us pinned down. They've also got a lot of our guns.'

Another shot rang out. Viall's men retreated down the street, keeping their heads down until they were out of range. But they had no sooner regrouped than a rifle bullet caught one of Viall's wranglers in the leg. As he went down, Murtagh saw a puff of smoke rising from behind the bell on the church roof. He loosed off a shot. There was a clang as the bullet hit the bell and spanged off harmlessly.

The attackers retreated again only to find themselves coming under withering fire from Whipple's general store. It was as if they were being deliberately herded. Flames spurted from the windows and bullets kicked up dust around the cowboys' feet. There were three more casualties.

'You stay here and keep them busy,' said Pat. 'I'll take a couple of men and go round the back. Maybe they're not so well defended in the rear.'

Viall ordered his men to take up positions which kept the front of the building covered. He sent a couple of men back to pin down the snipers on the roof of the hotel and the church. Once Viall's forces started firing back they felt better. They had no visible targets but at least they could keep Harker's men occupied.

A quick count revealed that Viall had nineteen men plus three wounded. Between them they had fifteen guns, including those of the men who had been shot. It wasn't enough firepower. He thought a moment, then called up Spence Colter and told him to go round to Judge Morton's house and tell him all bets were off unless he cooperated. The judge would know what that meant: the profitable arrangement he had with Viall, using the law to make his shady operations legal, would come to an end. The judge was a hunter, a regular guest at Viall's lodge on the old Dakins place. He had a whole armoury in his house. If he didn't break out some firepower, he would go down with Walter Viall.

'Don't forget: tell him 'all bets off',' said Viall. 'And say I ain't joking.'

The battle settled into a stalemate broken by sporadic gunfire.

Murtagh made his way through a gap between two buildings and ran along a dirt path that ran parallel to the main street which he crossed at a point hidden from snipers in the store and the church. Using the available cover, he and his two men crawled as near as they could to the rear of the stone emporium. The back was as solidly barricaded as the front. The rear doors looked firmly shut and probably had heavy merchandise piled against them. The windows were boarded up. Then he caught a movement high up, behind one of the chimneys. He reached for his carbine, took aim and fired.

There was a yell of surprise and a glimpse of a head around one side of the chimney. Murtagh fired again. This time there was no cry, only the sight of a body outlined against the sky for a moment before it crumpled, slid down the steep slope of the roof and hit the ground just in front of the loading bay doors.

Murtagh didn't stay to watch. He rolled to his left as fast as he could. A bullet from the roof from another sniper buried itself in the earth too close to his ribs for comfort. So they had snipers posted on the roof at the rear too. The two men with him were now blazing away. Further fire was returned from the stores. He told his men to stop shooting.

'They're hunkered down in there. They've got the place sealed up tight. You two stay here. Have a pot from time to time, just enough to let them know you're still around. That way you'll keep a couple of them busy.'

He crawled back on his belly until he was out of range then ran back the way he'd come to where Viall was dug in.

'The rear's clamped down tight, and the front's solid against us,' he said. 'This ain't going nowhere. We got to make something happen.'

'Like what?' said Viall. 'You got a pair of heavy cannon we can blow holes in those walls with?'

'No, but I remember a time in Tennessee, what was the name of the place, oh yes, Benson. You recall Benson?'

Viall's face lit up.

'Sure I recall Benson. Let's do it!'

★ ★ ★

Inside the store, the air was thick with the smell of cordite. Men were stationed at the windows peeking out through firing holes, fingers on triggers, waiting and watching for sight of a target, loosing off the occasional shot more out of frustration than with any real hope of hitting anything, for Viall's men were staying well hidden.

When Harker heard shots at the back of the store, he raced up the stairs to find out what was going on. He opened the roof window below the skyline and crawled over to where Sam Davis and Pete Jenkins were firing at targets that neither Harker nor they could see.

'They got Jimmy,' said Sam. 'Some shot it was too. He must only have shown an elbow but whoever it was surprised him then got him with a second bullet.

Harker frowned. Murtagh!

'I seen where it came from,' Sam went on, 'and I got a shot in too. Don't think I hit anything, though.'

'Go on keeping your heads down. Don't take any risks. Some of those men down there are professionals. They're real good and don't miss often. Don't get excited. Stay cool and return fire so they know to keep away.'

He ran back down to the ground floor. The situation had not changed. In the lull, he told the men to get themselves a drink and a smoke while they could. He looked through his spy-hole and scoured the street for signs of life. The front windows had been shot out but the sacks of flour and beans which did service for sandbags absorbed the bullets.

'My, my!' came a mocking voice at his back. 'It would take a clever man to say who is getting the best of this. Pa, who's trying to get in, or you who can't get out!'

'Stow it, Mikey,' said Billy.

'All Pa's got to do is sit tight and wait for you to come out,' said Rube. 'You can't stay in here for ever. Sooner or later you'll run out of ammo and water.

And when you break out, Pa'll be ready for you!'

Billy left his post at the window, crossed to the foot of the stairs where the two Viall boys sat with their hands and feet bound to keep them out of mischief and stood over Mikey.

'You're lucky I'm not a vengeful man, Mikey. Otherwise I'd push your front teeth down into your feet and shake your head until I heard your pea-brain rattle inside it. But I don't hit people who can't fight back any more than I lock up women against their will. So I'll just stuff this gag in your mouth for now and maybe get back to you later.'

Rube said nothing, just grinned. But even though he wasn't saying anything, Billy gagged him too. Then he joined Harker and peered out into the street.

'If the roles were switched and we were outside and Viall in here,' said Harker, 'what would your next step be?'

'He tried going round the back and that didn't do any good. So maybe a parley?'

'Nothing to parley about. Bridges burned on both sides. No going back for either of us.

'Then perhaps he'll sit it out. Mikey's right. We can't stay here for ever. And there's no cavalry going to ride to the rescue. Only way we're going so save our own skins is to beat him off ourselves.'

Herbie Morris pulled the trigger of his old carbine and gave a whoop.

'I got me a bandido!' he said.

There was a flurry of shots in return and then everything went quiet again.

Harker stiffened: 'Billy, you'd better take a look at this.'

Billy peered down the sights of his gun. There was a stir of activity at the top of the street by the church.

'Why ain't Spencer and Cartwright taking pot shots at them from the roof?' he said.

'Because they're not on the roof any more,' said Harker.

Billy looked again. Further up the street, on a level with the church, a cart was turning out of an alley. Two men were sitting on the driving seat. But they weren't holding any reins because, first, there was no need since there were no horses pulling the cart and, second, their hands were tied behind their back and their legs were lashed to the seat. Behind them were bales of hay.

'Spencer and Cartwright! Human shield!' murmured Billy, 'We can't shoot for fear of hitting our own men.'

Though there was nothing pulling it, the cart was moving slowly down the street towards the store.

'It's being pushed from behind. Viall's got his men working like oxen.'

'It would be lighter if they didn't have all that straw up back of it,' said Herbie Morris.

'The straw's the point,' said Billy. 'When they get nearer, they'll speed up and torch it. Then they'll run it into the storefront. I expect they'll have poured a couple or three gallons of resin from the sawmill over it. Should help spread the flames nicely.'

'You mean they're going to burn us out?' said Herbie.

Then things began to move fast. The cart speeded up, plumes of smoke started pouring out from the back, then bright red flames. Harker, Billy and the rest of the men in the store started pumping bullets at it, aiming low not just to miss Spencer and Cartwright but also because it was the only chance they had of hitting any of Viall's men at the back of it.

Smoke now filled the street. Harker saw Spencer who had somehow freed his arms, struggling to untie Cartwright. Then he lost sight of both in the smoke as the cart smashed into the storefront, spilling its load which began to burn fiercely. The stone of the walls and the barrier of sacks kept the flames at bay but soon the main door was ablaze. Smoke poured in, making the air difficult to breathe.

'We can't stay here,' yelled Billy above the noise.

'I just checked the rear,' said Harker.

'I reckon we'd stand a better chance making a break there than here. Herbie,' he called, 'go tell the boys we're going out the back way. Viall's got men waiting for us back there but not as many as out front, but that won't last. Tell Sam and Pete to stay on the roof as long as they can and give us covering fire.'

'What about these two?' asked Herbie, nodding to the Viall brothers.

'Cut them loose, but mind they don't get their hands on any guns,' said Harker who made his way through the smoke to the rear of the building where his men were dismantling the stack of merchandise piled high against the heavy double doors. Before pulling them open, he sent Herbie Morris to call down the men from the roof and posted a couple of fresh snipers in the ground floor windows to cover their break. Then, guns blazing, he led the way out of the store, which was now a blazing inferno.

Herbie Morris cut the rope around Mikey's hands then left him to untie his brother while he hurried off to join Harker in the back of the store.

Mikey freed Rube's hands and soon both were on their feet.

'Front way?' gasped Rube through the smoke.

Mikey nodded. They'd get a hotter reception if they followed Harker's men out through the back than if they made a dash for it through the blazing door.

Seizing whatever rags and cloths that came to hand, they wrapped their heads and hands to protect them against the searing heat then took off. As they emerged through the wall of flame, they shouted: 'Pa! It's us, don't shoot!'

They were met by a hail of bullets. Judge Morton had handed over his firearms which were being put to good use. Bullets and big-calibre slugs hit them from an assortment of weapons. But some came from the gun in Walter

Viall's fist. He recognized his boys a split second after he'd pulled the trigger. They were stopped in their tracks. He watched as they were driven back by the force of the fusillade into the flames.

★　★　★

Murtagh watched it happen. He knew that Harker wouldn't make the same mistake and would try to break out from the back. Barking orders at the reception party which were now positioned at the wrong side of the building, he ordered them round to the rear. But he was too late. The defenders had made their break. A few of them hadn't got far. They lay on the ground. But most were out and shooting back. Murtagh checked twice but neither Harker nor Billy were among the dead or wounded.

★　★　★

When he saw his two boys die, Walter Viall knew he'd lost not just the battle but the war. It wasn't grief that took the fight out of him because he'd never thought much of any of his sons. They weren't as smart as him; not one of them had what it took to take life by the throat and put his stamp on it. But somehow the deaths of Mikey and Rube coming so fast after Zeke had thrown his life away acting like a spoiled kid seemed a turning point. His instinct, which had never let him down, told him it was time to get out. He was finished in Laureston. He'd fouled his nest in a big way. His career in politics in Tate County was over before it had begun. No point in hanging on. Better to cut and run.

But he had no intention of going empty-handed.

12

Shootout

Walter Viall, once uncrowned king of Tate County, holstered his gun, snapped a few orders to cover his retreat and collected his horse from where he had tethered it outside the sheriff's office. But instead of taking off east along the trail to Santa Fe where no one knew him and he could make a fresh start, he rode the other way. He reined in at the blacksmith's, stayed inside for just five minutes, then moved on. He stopped outside Jepson's bank. It was locked. He used a bullet for a key and walked in. It was empty like everywhere else in Laureston. He strode past the counter into Old Man Jepson's office, stared at the safe and started untying the bag of blasting powder he'd got from Cy Biggar's smithy.

★ ★ ★

Behind the store, battle was raging. Harker's men had found good cover among the carts, stables and outbuildings in the back yard. Murtagh was working his men round to good counterattacking positions when he suddenly came under fire from his rear. He turned and saw that Sheriff Rukatch and three men, Harker's last-ditch reserve force, had him in their sights. Art Henderson, who was standing just next to him, suddenly gave a gasp and went down, blood pouring from a hit he'd taken in the chest. The rest of Viall's men turned at the same time and, realizing they were caught in a crossfire, started throwing down their guns, holding their arms in the air and shouting that they wanted to surrender.

As the firing died away, Murtagh seized his chance and ducked behind a low wall and ran along it unseen to the alley which brought him out in the main street. The store was still burning.

Two of Viall's boys were there, covering the front door but they weren't firing since nobody was coming out that way. Viall was nowhere in sight. He asked the men. They didn't know where he'd got to.

It was then that Murtagh reached the same conclusion as Walter Viall had come to only minutes before. Walt was finished in Laureston. Murtagh knew it made no sense to hang around and get stuck on the losing side of an argument that wasn't his anyway. He'd made up his mind to get out while he could when he heard a muffled explosion.

It didn't come from Whipple's store, though there was plenty there that might have gone up in the heat, but from the opposite direction. It also sounded further away than the hotel. That left the bank. It didn't take long to work out that the connection between 'bank' and 'explosion' meant someone had had the idea of lining his pockets while the population was elsewhere, the law was busy and no one would come to find out what all the fuss was about.

Murtagh marched up the empty main street. Once past the hotel, he advanced more cautiously, stopped thirty yards short of the bank and ran an eye over the place. A horse stood patiently at the hitching rail. The bank's front door was open. Moving as quietly as a latecomer in church, he tip-toed up the three steps to the entrance, listened, looked and went inside. He caught a scuffing noise behind the door which said 'Manager'. He kicked it open and saw Walter Viall pulling neat bundles of banknotes from a blown safe and stashing them in a saddle-bag.

'Running out on me, Walt?' he said.

'Getting out, yes, but not running out on you, Pat. Would I ever do such a thing? The game's up here, so I thought I'd get a stake together for us. I was going to come back and get you so we could shake the dust of Laureston from our feet and get back in business just like in the old days. Come on, give me a hand . . .'

He reached into the safe, brought out another package of dollar bills and thrust it into the bag. When he took his hand out of the bag, it had a gun in it. He didn't intend to share the money with anybody, nor was he going to pass up a chance of eliminating a witness to his past.

But it was no contest. He was just too slow. He was caught by a single shot that found his heart. Murtagh stood over him for a moment. Then he leaned down and pulled the bag away. No sense getting blood all over the money.

In the still-empty street, he hung the bag from the pommel of Viall's saddle, mounted his horse and dug his heels into its ribs. It took off fast down the street towards the western sky where the sun was low. Give it another hour and it would be dark, and dark is the bad man's friend.

As he passed the hotel, a rifle barked. Murtagh's horse faltered, recovered for a few strides and then went down, throwing him and rolling on the money bag which split, releasing dollar bills which blew and swirled and eddied like autumn leaves in a breeze.

As he got to his feet, he saw a sniper walk out on to the boardwalk outside the hotel. Before the carbine could bark a second time, Murtagh had got his shot in. The man gave a sigh, dropped his gun and fell. He didn't get up.

Murtagh looked around and when he was satisfied there were no other guns pointing at him, scooped up the money bag. He cut a length of rein from the dead horse's harness and wound it round and round the bag, closing the split so that no more money fell out. He looked up and down the street. He needed something else to ride.

He crept back towards the store. It was still burning. Viall's men had gone and the street was now deserted. Keeping in the lee of the buildings, he reached the turn-off to the sheriff's office where he'd hitched his own nag when Viall and the rest of his boys had left theirs. They were still there, waiting quietly, still saddled up. He threw the money bag over his horse's neck, unhitched the reins and was about to mount when a voice said:

'Hold it, Pat! You ain't going nowhere!'

Harker was fast on the draw, but Pat was faster. At the first sound of Harker's voice, he twisted away, ducked under his horse's belly and made a dash for Rukatch's porch. As he went, he half turned and fired. Harker felt a blow on the top of his left shoulder. It was no stronger than if he'd ridden too close to a sappy branch, but it made him dive for cover. He landed on his shot shoulder and almost yelled with the pain of it. No sappy branch had ever hurt like that.

Murtagh fired at the yell. Harker heard the slug zip past his ear and fired back. Then there was silence. Harker felt his shoulder. There was a lot of blood. But as far as he could tell, the bullet had clipped the fleshy outside of the joint and had missed the bone, leaving minimum damage.

He heard a shuffling sound. Harker shot at it, once in the centre of the sound then two more times, to the left and right of the spot. There was no sign he'd hit anything. How many slugs did he have left in the chamber? This was no time to start asking questions like that. Could he risk another peek? While he hesitated, Murtagh squirted out from the alley and, using the horse as cover, unhooked the money bag from his pommel. Again Harker fired. This time he knew for definite he had missed. He heard feet moving swiftly away down the alley and beyond the back of the sheriff's office.

Breaking cover, he set off in pursuit. His arm bothered him. It hung loose and hampered his movements. He stopped a moment to get a bearing on his quarry, but there was nothing to see and all he could hear was the rasp of his own breathing. He knelt behind a tree trunk until his breath slowed. He laid his six-shooter on the ground beside him and, one-handed, refilled the chamber with bullets from the loops in his belt. He snapped the chamber shut and felt better: it had been empty.

He marshalled his thoughts. He remembered that at the back of Rukatch's jail was a ridge which fell away steeply into a valley so densely wooded it could swallow the trail of a dozen fugitives. Not the sort of place to follow a man as quick with a gun as Murtagh. He backed a hunch and stayed put. Minutes went by. Then he heard a grunt and a curse and then saw a faint movement in the undergrowth. The slope had proved too steep and the brush too dense for Murtagh to get through and he was coming back. Harker waited for the right moment then fired. He was rewarded with a yell. Almost instantaneously his fire was returned and a bullet whanged off the tree trunk. He got off another shot and rolled to his right. He fetched up against another tree. He got round the back of it and crouched. He could hear Murtagh shuffling through last year's leaves maybe twenty yards ahead of him, but he couldn't see him.

'You got a choice, Murtagh. Throw your gun down or I'll kill you!'

'You'll have to come and get me, hot shot! But you take care. I'll be waiting and watching for you!'

Slowly, Harker worked his way through the brush towards the place the voice had come from. His shoulder was stiffening and he was losing blood fast. He gritted his teeth and pulled himself upright.

A bullet whined past his head and he dropped to the ground again. It was followed instantly by another shot and this time it felt as though someone had taken a hammer to his right leg. Finding cover behind a fallen log, he looked down at the wound. He'd been lucky again. The slug had scored the back of the calf, made a mess of the muscle but left the leg usable, just. Two good breaks. Was it going to be never two without three? Or third time unlucky?

Slowly he raised his head and looked over the log. He saw leaves and patches of dappled sun. Then the wind drew back a branch like a curtain and he caught a glimpse, thirty yards dead ahead, of the clapboard rear of Rukatch's jail. He also heard voices, mostly men's. The sheriff was back. The siege must be over and all Viall's boys had surely been rounded up or were dead. But there were women's voices too. He thought maybe Martha and Tabitha had come back to town with Doc Prentice from Breakjaw Creek.

But Murtagh, nursing his left hand which had been hit, had heard them too and realized the fix he was in. A welcoming committee with feelings that were less than warm stood between him and his horse. He'd have to make his move now, before Rukatch, Billy and half a dozen guns realized he was there. But surely they'd heard the gunfire at the back of the sheriff's office?

Harker was about to call out, to warn his friends that Murtagh was on the loose and ready to shoot the first thing that moved. But at that moment the wind riffled through the leaves again and gave him a brief but clear sight of his opponent. Raising his gun, he took aim and fired.

Murtagh was knocked on to his back by the force of the shot. But the bag of money he was still carrying blocked the bullet and left him winded but otherwise unhurt. He was up again before the first shock had passed. But his reactions took longer to recover and Harker got in a second shot. But his movements were clumsy too and the bullet, though it went home, did not stop his man. Murtagh went down again with a slug in the thigh. Harker hauled himself to his feet and stumbled across to Murtagh who lay bleeding and defenceless on the ground. Slowly he raised his gun which hung unsteadily from the end of his good arm. Murtagh groaned and sat up. He too raised his gun.

Harker's six-shooter had suddenly

become much too heavy to be lifted by one man. Anyway, his target wouldn't keep still but flickered and floated like a desert mirage. He couldn't get a shot in. But he saw Murtagh's gun come up and point at him and knew he'd played his last play. Third time unlucky it was, then. A gun roared. He saw flame at the end of the barrel of Murtagh's gun.

Harker waited for the bullet. It was a long time coming, so long that he didn't have the strength to go on standing upright to wait for it for long. His knees crumpled, but what the hell, he could wait for it just as well sitting on the ground as standing up.

He waited some more but the bullet didn't come. Pat was getting up and taking a long time doing it. He was bleeding from the thigh and his right hand. Harker watched him climb to his feet slowly. It was like watching weeds waving in a river current. He saw Murtagh's head tilt back unhurriedly and the gush of red on his temple. There was a look of amazement in his eyes as he slowly subsided, bounced gently twice on the ground and then stopped moving at all.

Harker's eyes were suddenly obscured, filled by a blur. He screwed them up and the blur snapped clear and resolved into the face of Tabitha. In her hand was a smoking gun.

'Even a woman with a murdered husband doesn't shoot the man who murdered him in the back,' she said. 'But if she's got any spark in her, she won't pass up the chance of getting justice.'

And then there were people and hands that carried him into the light and whiskey wiped the remaining cobwebs away from the back of his eyes and eased the pain while Doc Prentice cleaned and bandaged his wounds.

* * *

The very next day the people of Laureston started putting their town back together again. The stores had to be set to rights, the hotel to be made fit to re-open, there were questions to be to put to Judge Morton, land deeds to be undone and restitutions made . . .

By the time the bunting was hung six weeks later over Whipple's shiny new store and the celebrations came to an end, Tom Harker was as good as new. He stayed for a spell out at Bluewater with Billy Boden, his old army comrade. Tabitha came out to see them. Abe came with her as often than not, for they were walking out. Grateful townspeople asked Harker if he'd take over the old Dakins place, make a go of it. But he wasn't tempted and one day, at the start of spring, he tied his bedroll to the back of his saddle and, riding tall and easy, he headed out along the road that wound through Mason Canyon.

This time, no one shot at him.

We do hope that you have enjoyed reading this large print book.

Did you know that all of our titles are available for purchase?

We publish a wide range of high quality large print books including:
Romances, Mysteries, Classics
General Fiction
Non Fiction and Westerns

Special interest titles available in large print are:
The Little Oxford Dictionary
Music Book, Song Book
Hymn Book, Service Book

Also available from us courtesy of Oxford University Press:
Young Readers' Dictionary
(large print edition)
Young Readers' Thesaurus
(large print edition)

For further information or a free brochure, please contact us at:
Ulverscroft Large Print Books Ltd.,
The Green, Bradgate Road, Anstey,
Leicester, LE7 7FU, England.
Tel: (00 44) **0116 236 4325**
Fax: (00 44) **0116 234 0205**

THE LAST GUNDOWN

Matt James

A town without mercy, a land without heart or soul: that was what bounty hunter Shell Dunbar confronted during that endless blazing summer. Even the handful of men who supported him gave him no chance of surviving that murderous summer of hate. They had already given him up for dead when he faced the last gundown . . .

DEATH RIDER

Boyd Cassidy

Mountain man Rufas Kane discovers Dan Cooper's dead body on a hillside overlooking the town of Death, leaving the townsfolk wondering why anyone would kill a harmless cowboy. Then one of Gene Adams' cowboys is killed in a gunfight with the ruthless Trey Skinner. It becomes apparent that Skinner is responsible for Cooper's death. But nothing's as it seems. That night, amid a spate of killings, Gene Adams vows to find the killer before dawn, or to die trying.

BIG TROUBLE AT FLAT ROCK

Elliot Long

Callum Bowden stared down at his adoptive father, John McKendry, lying dead in his coffin. He could barely look at the lifeless face and the silk wrapping that covered the ghastly wound across the throat ... Meanwhile, hatred had overwhelmed Jim McKendry, who swore that someone would pay for his father's death: no matter what it took, the killer would be brought to justice — alive or dead.

RANGELAND JUSTICE

Rob Hill

Jack Just, weary from long days on the trail, rides into an isolated cattle town on the Texas panhandle. There he finds that the greedy and powerful Clovis Blacklake has the town in his pocket. But when Jack also discovers that Blacklake has cheated the town's most downtrodden inhabitant out of his rightful property, he decides to make a stand. It takes a real man to fight the ruthless Blacklake; and when Jack does, the tables begin to turn . . .